T0067125

KEN WILBUR

authorHOUSE®

AuthorHouse™
1663 Liberty Drive
Bloomington, IN 47403
www.authorhouse.com
Phone: 1 (800) 839-8640

Published by AuthorHouse 03/18/2015

ISBN: 978-1-5049-0128-4 (sc)
ISBN: 978-1-5049-0127-7 (e)

Print information available on the last page.

. . . .

A Special Thank You for Their Art Work:

Angee Wilbur, my daughter, a graduate of Wayne State College, with a degree in art.

Alec Cadwell, an eighth grade student at Wylie Jr. High in Abilene, Texas

****

To Rachel Rosenboom a huge thank you for proof reading this novel.

CHAPTER ONE

Wade stood on the porch, gazing upon the Colorado valley he called his home, he remembered his father's words from long ago, "Nothing bad happens in this world that some good doesn't come of it." He guessed that was so very true in his case.

He would never forget the feeling of seeing what had once been his house, a home with white pillars, cotton and tobacco fields, nothing but charred rubble after the war. The Civil War was over but the South would never be the same. Both armies had lived off the land, what they didn't take and burn the White Trash that followed them had.

Had it not been for the War and the fact that his home in Tennessee was reduced to rubble, his parents both dead, he would not have any of this. He would not have meet Judith, and have Chet and Sarah who were playing in their tree house just around the corner.

He noticed a half dozen horses grazing near the head of the valley. Building a fence across the five hundred yards of the opening had been on his and Sweeny's "To do List" for months. It was one of the many things they didn't ever seem to find time to get done.

Judith's call to supper, snapped Wade back to the here and now.

He turned and called to Chet and Sarah to come and get washed up.

After they had finished eating and the table was cleared, Chet asked his dad to tell a story. Chet and Sarah loved to hear stories of when their father was a boy or of the Indians that roamed the plains.

"Long, long ago there lived as old warrior. He was very swift at running and very strong; no warrior in his tribe was his equal. His son was a good and kind boy, but he was not like his father. He was neither strong nor swift."

"The father forced his son to join in the games with the other Indian boys and to go with them on the hunts. It came time for the boy to make his first fast, to go without food. If he could fast longer than any of the other boys, perhaps the Master of Life would make him a great leader."

"Why did they do that?" Sarah asked.

"It was just their custom," Wade explained as he went on with his story. "The father built a fasting-lodge, and his son began to fast. Each day the father came to encourage his son. The boy wanted to break the fast. His father would not listen to his son's pleading. The other young men were giving up, he knew his son could do better, he could achieve greatness. He must be willing to make a greater sacrifice than all the others."

"What's a sacrifice?" Sarah asked.

"A sacrifice is to give up something. In this case it was going without food, having nothing to eat," Wade explained.

"So the father told him to last it out and not give up. The next morning all the other Indian boys had given up. He was the last. His father hurried to the boy's fasting lodge, carrying food for his son. But nearing the lodge, he heard the boy speaking."

"I have obeyed my father and the Master of Life has ended my suffering. The father ran to his son and cried, No, No, my son, do not leave me!"

"Do not regret this father, I was not put here to be a great warrior. We are created as the Master of Life thinks best. The boy raised his arms over this head and he disappeared through the smoke-hole at the top of the lodge. He was never seen again."

"What happened to him?" Chet asked. His eyes as big as silver dollars.

"Well, when his father left the lodge, he saw a bird perched on a tree limb singing a new melody. No one had ever seen this bird before, it had a red-breast and brown body and sang a sweet sound. The bird was the red-breasted Robin. And since that day, the Robin has been a friend to all men. He lives near their lodges and receives food from them; no man ever turns his weapon toward the Robin."

"When we die, do we come back as a bird or animal?" Chet wanted to know.

"Some people believe that we do."

"What do you believe, dad?" Sarah asked.

"I and your mother believe in Jesus, that he will take us to Heaven when we die. Now, get ready for bed and remember to say your prayers." Wade gave Chet a pat on his rear to get him moving.

"Wade Wilbur, you're going to fill those kid's heads full of all kinds of nonsense. Between you and Music. I heard Chet trying to sing the words to, 'Preacher and the Bear' the other day when he didn't think anyone was around." She had to admit, that she too kind of enjoyed listening to the stories and hearing Music sing his songs.

"They both have enough of you in them to offset any bad influence that Music or I may give them."

"What's that supposed to mean?" Judith asked with a look that said, be very careful how you answer that.

"That means, that you are a good thing, a very good thing." Wade gave her a pat on her tooch that made her jump like a young school girl.

It is not so much what we have in life, but who we have in our life that matters, and Wade felt very blessed.

CHAPTER TWO

"We lost some horses last night, I will be leaving as soon as I tell Sweeny, and can you fix me up some grub to take."

"Do you think they were rustled?" Judith asked with a worried tone.

"Don't know. We do need to get a fence up at the mouth of the valley, saw a half dozen head grazing near there last evening. If they were rustled it may take a few days, if they just drifted off, I will be back by noon."

She hated it when he went off like this, the waiting was the hardest part. She knew it was necessary but that didn't make it any easier.

"Maybe I should tell you before you leave that I am real sure now." She watched to see his expression.

"Real sure of…..?" Wade didn't finish.

"Real sure that Chet and Sarah are going to have a little brother or sister." She replied with a smile.

"You are! Hey, that's great!" They had talked about it and thought that it would be nice to have the third child.

"You sorry you married me, you ever wished you had married Penny?"

"Judith, you are the best thing that ever happened to me, I couldn't be happier." He went to her and took her in his arms.

"Why don't you ever tell me that? Why do I always have to ask?"

Wade looked down into her eyes, kissed her upper lip and then on both of her full lips. "Guess I just take you for granted, thinking that you know how I feel about you, how lucky I consider myself to have you for my partner."

Judith smiled, her full lips framing glistening white teeth. "I do know that you love me, but a gal likes to hear it said once in a while."

"I promise to do better," Wade said as he picked up the sack she had made for him. "Be back as soon as I can and will do my best to show you just how special you are to me." He said with a little chuckle.

He was wearing his Colt on his right hip and on his left hip he carried the special shotgun pistol he had made years ago in Missouri. The gunsmith had done an excellent job, the weapon had balance and enough fire power to clear a room with one squeeze of the trigger. He also had his Henry in the scabbard on his saddle. He hoped he would not have to use any of his weapons, but knew it was necessary to have them, just in case. It was tough, hard times. Gold had been discovered in Colorado in 1859 and the fever of it got a hold of the minds of men.

For some it was a fabulous fortune, for others it was a hard life and an early grave. Prices soared to great heights in the gold fields. A plate of bacon and eggs could cost five dollars, an old newspaper sold for a dollar. A tree limb and rope served as swift punishment for the two unforgivable crimes, claim jumping and horse stealing.

Rustlers knew this and for this reason, they would fight and shoot to kill. He had to be careful not to ride into an ambush. Wade didn't know for sure that the horses had been rustled, they could have drifted with the wind during the night. He hoped that was the case. Because two of those missing were two year old off-spring of the big black he was riding, Wade did not want to lose them. Wade had traveled from Tennessee with Blue Eagle, a Tennessee Walking Stallion his father had raised.

Blue Eagle was beginning to get a little long in the tooth, soon it would be time to find another stud. They had a couple of his son's that they didn't geld and were using on a few mares, but they talked of getting a new stud to cross with his off-spring.

Mounting the big black, he rode to the mouth of the valley to pick up sign. He would soon know if they just drifted off or if they had been driven.

He picked up the sign without any problem and what he feared was revealed to be true. The horses were being driven by two riders. One a great deal smaller than the other. Wade could tell by the size of the horse and the weight of the horse and rider. The bigger man and horse made a much clearer track. The horse was in need of being shod. His right front shoe was worn very badly and the imprint showed the horse threw the foot a little different. The other set of tracks were fainter but they too, told a story. The horse tended to walk on his toes in the rear.

The tracks led west toward the foothills of the Rockies. This was wild country. Wade had hoped they would head for Denver but this was not the case. In Denver he could get help from the law and his brand was well known so he would have no trouble at all defending his story. In the foothills he would have to be his own law.

Wade followed the tracks to where they had camped for the night. Looking at the sun he knew they had several hours and many miles on him. He let the black drink at the small stream, while he took some jerky and thought over the situation. He knew his black could walk faster than the average horse but he worried most about riding into an ambush. In riding to overtake them, he could ride right into the business end of a rifle. These foothills offered more places to set up an ambush than he could count.

They were headed away from Denver. In the general direction of Clear Creek, Fairplay or Leadville. Wade had not been to any of these small mining towns but he heard of them. The tracks led around several small lakes nestled in the mountains. Lodgepole Pine and Aspen were numerous making it difficult to see very far ahead. It would be slow work tracking them in this country. He watched a Rocky Mountain Jay and Hermit Thrush play in a spruce tree as he planned his next move. He remembered that Clear Creek was more to the northwest and the tracks had turned south. Fairplay was about forty miles through the foothills. By going around, it would be longer but Wade liked the idea of them coming to him, rather than riding into an ambush. Mounting the black he turned southeast to ride around the rough country and get ahead of the rustlers.

"If they change direction and head to Clear Creek we can kiss those horses good-bye," he said to Eagle. Wade would often talk to his horse as if he were human, many riders shortened the lonely hours in the saddle singing or talking to their horses.

Now that he didn't have any tracks to follow, he could travel at night. It would get dark early in the foothills, and the rustlers would have to camp for the night.

Later that night Wade topped a ridge and saw the many campfires of Fairplay dotting the hill side, still several miles away. Dawn made a pale reddish light in the east as Wade built a coffee-making fire. He would wait for them to come down out of the foothills. That is, if he had guessed right. If he had guessed wrong they would be long gone and he would be out six head of his best stock.

Wade rubbed down Eagle and after giving him some grain, staked him out on a patch of lush grass. Eagle would be out of sight to anyone coming down from the north. Wade didn't want them to see Eagle before he saw them. The brand, an eagle head on the left rear hip, would give him away sure as Hell. All the horses wore the brand. A blacksmith in St. Louis had made the branding iron for him and it was a very good likeness of an eagle head.

Wade drank coffee, fixed some breakfast and waited. This was the hard part, the waiting. Wade had never been good at waiting. Minutes dragged, the sun was up and Wade drifted off to sleep. He didn't know how long he slept but the sound of iron on rock made him snap awake. There he heard it again, the sound of a horseshoe on rock. Someone was coming out of the foothills. From the sound he knew it was more than two horses. They were still several hundred yards away, but there was no mistaking the sounds.

In moments, two men appeared each leading three horses. They were young, neither of them was over sixteen. They both had guns tied down on their hips. Both were dressed for comfort and utility, not style. Their tight-fitting blue canvas pants made them look skinny. They did not fit the picture Wade had in his mind of the rustlers. He pictured them as dirty, ugly, misfits. These two looked like anything but that. They looked like they should be attending a church social, not stealing horses.

"Hello camp," one of them yelled. Wade rolled up on one elbow to get a better look. Neither of them expected Wade to be the owner of the horses they had. Both were toe-headed and had never shaved.

Wade added some fuel to the fire and waved for the two horse thieves to enter camp. He leaned back against his saddle and relaxed as they tied their horses to some brush at the edge of camp.

"Got some coffee if you got cups," Wade called. He watched them as they each took a tin cup from their saddle bags.

"Lose your horse?" The young blond doing the talking looked like anything but a horse thief. "Got some extra ones, if you got the price."

"Be stupid to buy my own horses," Wade had his Colt beside him under the saddle blanket.

Surprise showed on their faces. "You calling us horse thieves?"

Wade thought for a second they were both going for their guns, but for one reason or another, they didn't.

"Didn't call you anything. But those horses with the Eagle Brand, belong to me. How did you happen to come by them?" His voice was soft and low, but carried in it a sound of confidence.

"Bought them in Golden, got a bill-of-sale too." He started to reach in his vest picket but was stopped by the sound of Wade's voice.

"Those horses never been to Golden." The young man's hand seemed to be suspended in air. Calling a man a liar was reason to fight but he didn't know if it was reason enough to die. There was something about this man that told him not to make any sudden moves.

"I tracked those horses from my place, north of Denver, they never been near Golden." Wade wondered if there was going to be a way out of this. He could not see these two swinging from a low branch. He worried about getting them frightened and them going for their guns. He didn't want to push them too far and have to kill them or get himself killed. He wasn't going to wait any longer and give them a chance. All at once his Colt was leveled on them, hammer thumbed back.

"Just touch those guns and you're dead." With his left hand he drew the big shotgun pistol and leveled it. "Now, with your left hand unbuckle those belts and let them drop." He watched as they untied the rawhide, unbuckled the gun-belts and let them drop to the ground.

Wade never moved, his guns remained trained on the chests of the two young men. "Now, move away from them. Take a seat." He said as he pointed to the other side of the small campfire. "Tell me about yourselves, and keep it truthful."

"We came out from Ohio, ran out of money and they kicked us off the wagon train." The young men were both white as sheets and beads of sweat had formed on their faces. "We thought we could round up some wild horses but didn't have any luck. We were out of supplies, heading for Denver when we rode up on these six horses and thought it would be easy to turn them into ready cash."

"Don't you know a rope is administered as swift punishment for horse stealing?" Wade watched now as they looked at each other, fear masking their faces.

"You going to hang us mister?" The words got softer until you could hardly hear the last syllable.

CHAPTER THREE

Little Chet awoke in the middle of the night. Judith heard him cry and went to his bed side. She knew how much he missed his father and thought he must have had a bad dream. But when she put her hand on his forehead, she knew he was burning up with fever. He complained of being cold and his muscles were aching, but it was the fever that worried Judith.

She got a basin of water and a cloth to bathe his forehead. Rubbing the cool wet cloth on his arms and legs seemed to help, but the fever was still high and at times he would be nauseous. Judith worked with him until almost dawn. Telling him she would be right back, she ran over to Mc Sweeny's to get help.

"Sorry to wake you but Chet is real sick. He has a high fever and the chilies." Judith told Sweeny when he answered the door.

"Be right over Judith." He got his clothes and boots on while telling his wife Penny what was going on. In a few minutes Penny was also on her way. They took turns, putting cold cloths on Chet but the fever remained high and now he complained of a severe headache. The bright morning sunlight coming in his east window hurt his eyes and nothing they did seemed to help.

I better ride to Denver and get the doctor." Sweeny started for the door. "I will be back as soon as I can." With that he ran to get his horse. Moments later he rode hard down the valley toward Denver.

"Would you take Sarah over to your place Penny I don't know what this is but I don't want her to get it if we can help it." Judith continued to work on Chet.

"Sure, Jake and Dusty will be getting up, after I get them some breakfast, I can leave Jake in charge and come back to help you."

They worked with Chet all that day, he didn't want anything to eat but they forced him to sip on some broth and drink as much water as he could. His temperature remained high. They didn't know what else they could do for him. Judith wished Wade would get home. He had been gone for two days and she was beginning to worry about him.

"The hardest part of being a woman is waiting, it seems like I have spent half my life waiting." Penny had made some coffee and now handed Judith a cup.

"Yes, and I am very poor at it too." Judith took the coffee and sipped it. "It came on sudden like, he was feeling fine when he went to bed."

"That's the way with some things, they hit all at once." Penny put her hand on Chet's neck. "Temperature seems to be about the same. I don't think it is any higher."

"That's what I thought too." Judith replaced the wet cloth on Chet's forehead and pulled the blanket up around him. "I hope Dusty and Sarah don't catch it. They were together all day yesterday."

"I will go over to our place and check on them," Penny said as she started for the door.

Judith worked over Chet all day. He seemed to be best when she was reading to him.

It was almost sundown when she heard horses. Going to the window she saw Sweeny and the doctor. They were both in the doctor's buckboard, with Sweeny's horse tied on behind.

The doctor checked Chet, listened to his chest and asked him and Judith questions.

"Looks to be tick-fever. It is transmitted through the bite of a wood tick. Onset is sudden, will last about two-three days and disappear. But the remission will last only for a day or two and is usually followed by a second attack. The second attack most always is worse than the first. Nothing I can do, no treatment but what you are doing." He was picking up his things and putting them in his black bag.

Penny had made supper, so they all sit down to eat. Sweeny had not eaten all day and was about to die from hunger.

"Being it is so late, I will spend the night and keep an eye on him," doc was finishing his coffee. The meal had been delicious and with his pipe lit, he did not feel like going out again that night.

"If it is the tick-fever, he should feel better in the morning. Fever should be down and he should feel like eating. It is not contagious, the other children and you ladies will get it only if you are bitten by the wood tick." Doc was enjoying his pipe and coffee.

"But you say he will have a second attack following a day or two?" Judith felt much better now that the doctor had looked at Chet.

"Yes, and the second attack can be harder than the first." Judith poured him some more coffee.

"Just keep wet cloths on him and force liquids?" Penny asked.

"Yes, that is all that we know of to do." Doc puffed his pipe. "He's strong. Shouldn't be any problem, but he will be a sick boy for a few days."

Chet was at the table eating breakfast with doc and Sarah when Sweeny stopped in to see how he was doing.

"Well, you look much better this morning," Sweeny took the cup of coffee Judith handed him and joined them at the table.

"That's the way of the fever, comes all at once and leaves just as sudden." Doc was enjoying his breakfast. Judith was a good cook and the steak, eggs, potatoes, toast and homemade jams were as good as doc had eaten. Sweeny couldn't pass up the toast and jam even though he had just got up from the breakfast table at home.

"Got your team all hitched. Thought you would be wanting to get an early start." Sweeny said helping himself to more toast and blackberry jam.

"Yes, I got to be getting." Doc lit his pipe and started for the door. "You take it easy, drink lots of water and clean up your plate." He rubbed Chet's hair, took his bag and headed for his buckboard.

"Thanks again doc for coming out." The two dollars he charged didn't seem like enough to Judith. She would have paid ten times that amount.

The remission lasted a little more than a day. The fever was back and the aches and pains were more severe than before. Chet was burning up with fever and every time he moved his muscles and joints ached. He didn't cry much. Everyone including Chet seemed to feel better knowing what it was and that in a day or two it would be over.

Late that afternoon, the barking of the dog told Judith someone was coming. Going to the window she could see three riders coming down the valley floor. She recognized Blue Eagle and his rider. Going to the door, she ran to meet them. When Wade saw her he put his heels to Eagle and came at a run. Jumping from Eagle at the hitch rail, Wade took Judith in his arms and lifted her off her feet. She started to say something but his kiss quieted her and she relaxed and enjoyed the embrace. Clasped in his arms, she told him of Chet.

"Chet has tick-fever. The doc was here and he is okay but suffering. He will be as happy to see you as I was." Arm in arm they went to the cabin. Just before going into the cabin Wade stopped and turned to speak to the two men with him. "Put my horse in the barn, rub him down and take care of the gear."

They nodded agreement and he went inside with Judith. Sarah came running, jumping into his arms with her arms locked around his neck.

"Doc said it was not contagious. That it had to be transmitted by the bite of a wood tick. So Sarah came home. At first she was over at Sweeny's with Jake and Dusty." She took Sarah from Wade.

"Hey, what's this I hear about my little man being sick?" Wade took Chet into his arms and he could feel the fever in his body. Chet felt better having his father hold him, and after a while he dropped off to sleep, something he had not been able to do. At the table with Sarah on his lap and coffee he told everyone of tracking the rustlers. He sent Jake to the barn to fetch the two men.

"It was either turn them loose, leave them to hang or bring them back with me. They're young, brothers that got off on the wrong foot. I don't think they are bad, but I didn't want to just turn them loose after what they did. They do need some help and we got something's that they can help us with." They all looked up as Jake and the two young men entered.

"This is Tom and Tim Harper. They are going to build us a fence across the mouth of the valley. This is my wife Judith, Penny, and Sweeny. We have two more, Chet who is not feeling well and his sister Sarah. That red head belongs to Sweeny and Penny and his name is Dusty you have already met Jake." The boys nodded to each and shifted from one foot to the other in a nervous fashion. They didn't seem to know what to do with their hands. "You boys go fix yourselves up some bunks in the tack room. Sweeny and I will be out in a while." Wade watched as they hurried out. "Oh, I am so glad you didn't leave them to hang. They look like nice young men." Judith poured more coffee and they shared experiences.

CHAPTER FOUR

Wade and Sweeny walked into the tack room and found the boys working to make it suitable for sleeping. They had two bunks against one wall.

"Have a seat boys. Sweeny and I have some things to go over with you." Wade motioned for them to take a seat on their bunks.

"Just want you to understand what is expected of you and what you can look forward to from us," Sweeny added.

The boys nodded. Both had trouble looking Wade and Sweeny in the eye. They knew they were lucky to still be alive.

"Tim, you will take your meals with the McSweeney's and Tom you'll eat at my place. The first two weeks you are on probation. You work without pay. If at the end of two weeks, you want to stay on, and we want to keep you, the pay's twenty-five a month plus your board and room." Both boy nodded as Wade paused.

"We want a day's work for a day's wage," Sweeny added.

"I know you won't, but should you run off before the two weeks are up." Again Wade paused. "We'll come after you and you will not be happy."

"You needn't worry about us running off, we are just thankful for the chance you have given us."

Wade handed them their gun belts, "Better wear these, but don't use them unless you are forced to." Wade opened the door and walked out.

"How good are you with your guns?" As he asked the question, he picked up some hunks of wood and placed them against the canyon wall. They stepped back twenty yards or so.

"Guess we're as good as most," Tim replied.

"Draw and shoot those hunks of wood."

Both young men drew and shot from the hip, neither of them hit the targets. Taking more time and holding the gun at arm's length, they both scored a hit. They stepped back and looked to Wade and Sweeny for approval.

Wade whipped out his Colt and fired. The slug sent one of the hunks of wood flying. Wade's second shot, followed so closely that the two explosions sounded as one, hitting the small target in mid-air and slamming it against the canyon wall.

Tim nudged Tom and whispered, "See that, if we would have drawn on him we would be cold in our graves right now."

"Sweeny's no great artist with his hand gun but with his saddle rifle he can knock a whisker off a mountain lion at two hundred yards." Wade reloaded his Colt and dropped in back into his holster.

"Your first job will be to build a fence of Lodgepole Pine across the mouth of the valley. You cut the poles from the bluffs, drag them down, dig the post holes, and build a good two rail fence," Sweeny said. "Any questions?"

"Just show us where to find the tools, we will take it from there." Sweeny went with them and showed them where all the tools were, what horses they could use and answered their few questions. Wade had hurried back to help Judith with Chet and Sarah.

The days passed fast for Tim and Tom as they worked from sun up to sun down. It was hard work, but they did a good job and looked upon the finished product with pride. They put in a nice gate with two high side poles. From the cross-beam they hung a sign, "Eagle Valley". It was burned into a two inch plank of Spruce. With six inch letters, it could be read from fifty yards away.

At breakfast, they asked Wade and Sweeny to ride down and inspect their work. They were proud of it and wanted to be there when they saw it for the first time.

It was a nice day so Judith and Penny packed a lunch and they took the buckboard. They were all in the buckboard except Jake, he rode his paint pony and raced on ahead. The boys were just putting on the finishing touches and picking up their tools when they pulled up.

The fence was nice, it not only was solid and useful but it added some class to the ranch. It was impressive.

"Why Eagle Valley?" Judith asked.

"Well," Tim started, "Your brand for one thing, the Eagles up on the bluffs, and." He paused. "The Eagle is strong and powerful, just like this ranch."

"I like it," Penny put in. "What do you guys think?" She said as she looked from Sweeny to Wade.

They both just nodded and smiled. The boys had done a good job, they had worked hard, had not asked a question every time they turned around but went ahead and did what had to be done. They were both happy.

It had not been all work for Tim and Tom, Wade had sent them hunting from time to time. He gave each of them a mustang and helped them to break it. He also worked with them on shooting. He figured if a man was going to carry a gun, he better know how to use it. Some men take to shooting faster than others. A lot of it depends on hand-eye coordination, agility, and quickness. But a great deal comes with practice, practice until the gun was an extension of the hand. The boys improved a great deal, but they could practice all day for a year and never be as quick and sure with a six gun as Wade was.

The weeks passed fast and Tim and Tom had become a part of the family of Eagle Valley. It had been years since they had felt a part of anything. They were happy. One Saturday morning, Wade and Sweeny gave each of them a twenty dollar gold piece and told them to have a good time in Denver. The boys didn't require any nudging, they cleaned up and were riding toward Denver within an hour.

"Think they will be back?" Sweeny asked as they watched them ride down the valley.

"I'd bet my last dollar on it".

Denver was a maze of activity, people hurrying everywhere. The saloons, dance halls, and gambling dens all beckoned them to throw away their hard earned money. This easy money, attracted men and women alike to Denver. Denver was growing daily. In the 1870's, it is estimated that the railroad brought 100 new residents to Denver each day. The population of Denver grew from 4,759 in 1870 to over 35,000 by 1880.

Both Tim and Tom lacked the knowledge to compete with the people after their money. They were innocent to the ways of frontier towns.

Their first stop was the general store where they each got a new shirt and a pair of socks. Their next stop was the Red Dog Saloon. They ordered Kentucky bourbon, but they got corn whiskey made in Denver not more than a week ago. They sipped their whiskey and watched the people. The saloon girls were ugly, repulsive. Even being scantily dressed did little or nothing for them.

One of them, old enough to be their mother, spotted them and came their way. Her hair was lemon-colored, her breasts pushed against her flimsy dress revealing everything she had. Tom watched the rising and falling with each breath. When she began to fondle him, he was nervous as a fox in a forest fire.

"Hi cowboy, wanta buy a thirsty gal a drink?" She was disgusting and Tom didn't want anything to do with her. Drinking his whiskey in one gulp, he almost choked as it burned all the way down. He grabbed Tim and almost ran from the saloon.

They went to another bar and this time ordered a beer. It was only sundown and at this rate they would both be under the table before the Saturday night activities even got a good start. The bartender made them a little uneasy. He was, or had been a brawler, his face showed that his nose had been broken and his brows were lumpy. His neck was as big around as his fat jowls were wide.

"You boys just get into town?" His voice didn't seem to go with his face. It was rather pleasant.

"Yep, work for a ranch north of here." Tim said it with pride. They both had been happier the last month than at any time in their lives.

"Well, if ya want anything ya can't find, just let me know." He gave the boys a crooked smile and went to the other end of the bar to take care of a customer.

The boys moved to a table to watch the activity going on around them. Miners, storekeepers, gamblers, and cowboys much like themselves were playing cards or just talking and drinking. Most seemed to be happy-go-lucky types, but a few reminded them of a grizzly, mean with temper and strength to make them dangerous.

"Be an easy place to get into trouble," Tim said. His tongue was getting thick, making his speech a little slurred.

"Without even trying," Tom agreed.

The men at the next table were talking about the Shawnee Trail that branched off and led to Junction City, Kansas. A herd of Texas cattle were on their way north. They talked of the great demand for cattle here in Denver, and how a man could make good money buying cattle in Kansas and bringing them on up to Denver.

"Both Fort Logan and Fort Morgan need cattle, to say nothing of what Denver needs." The man speaking looked like he could be a banker.

"Yes, and the older cows could be used to start a cow-calf herd." The boys listened with interest. They knew Wade and Sweeny had been talking of buying some cattle.

"Those Texans are ready to sell when they hit Kansas, the last thing any of them want to do is to drive the herd on northwest to Denver."

"True, and the hardest part of the trip is from Texas to Kansas, over the dry plains." The banker looking man shifted his cigar from hand to hand as if it were a hot branding iron.

"Usually within a few hours of delivering the cattle to the stockyards, the drovers are deep in fun or deep in trouble. Those cattle towns like Abilene, Wichita, Miles City, or in this case, Junction City are wild and woolly to say the least."

The boys listened to them talk, but couldn't hear every word. The whiskey and beer had dulled their minds, making their perception a little slow. But they continued to listen, hoping to remember so they could pass it on the Wade and Sweeny.

An old-timer who looked like a copy of what the boys pictured a Pony Express rider to look like took a chair at their table. Skinny, wiry, his pants were tucked into his boot tops, and his hat was held in place with a piece of rawhide. His hair was white and it fell almost to his shoulders. His mustache too was so gray that it looked white except for the stains by the corners of his mouth. He spat a string of tobacco juice at the brass spittoon, hitting the receptacle dead center.

"You young bucks buy me a drink and I'll give you some words of wisdom worth twice the price." His deep set beady eyes darted from Tom to Tim and back again.

"Sure, why not?" Tom went to the bar and returned with a shot for the old-timer.

He took the whiskey, threw back his head and poured the shot down as if it were water. Taking his finger, he wiped out the shot glass and licked his finger.

"Nothing but trouble here. Get on up the street. Half of these guys would kill for your clean shirts." Without saying another word he got up and made his way through the crowd to another table with a couple of cowboys sitting at it.

The boys looked at each other. Tom motioned toward the swinging doors and Tim nodded. All at once they both felt like they needed some fresh air. The stale smell of smoke, whiskey and body odor hung in the air like a tent over their heads. Once outside, they both felt much better.

"I could use something to eat," Tim said.

"Me too," Tom replied as he led the way toward the business section of Denver.

Walking past the various shops, Tom noticed a sign in one of the windows. "Box Social, and its tonight. Maybe that's a place where we can get some good food and meet some girls."

"Says it's at the church, we ain't been in a church for years."

"So what?" Tim took Tom by the arm and they started down the street. "Better than ending up with one of those worn out women or worse."

"True, but let's look things over, we don't want to rush into anything."

They found the church, a white frame building with a tall white cross on the front. There were several buggies and saddle horses tied outside. Half block away the boys could hear the auctioneer. "Two, I got two, who will make it two-an-a-quarter." He spoke so fast and ran the words together in a sing-song way that made it hard to understand.

They mounted the steps and looked in through the window of the big front door. The auctioneer was up front with a table full of fancy boxes.

He was holding one in his hand and singing his song to several young men, trying to get one of them to bid. From the looks of things, there were more boxes than there were men to buy them.

The boys eased through the door, not wanting to draw any attention to themselves. The church was bright, the pews pushed against the walls. Were filled with young ladies waiting for someone to buy their box and share the lunch. The auctioneer sold the box he held and picked up another off the table to take bids on. Box after box was sold and the number of young men bidding was cut considerable as the couples went to the benches to enjoy their lunch. "Oh, looky here," the auctioneer cried. "Here's a pretty one, and it smells like fried chicken. Who will start the bidding at five dollars, I want six. Okay, I'll let everyone in. A dollar bill, I want two, who will give me two, I got one, give me two," he cried. Tim said something to Tom and Tom nodded his head. The auctioneer seeing this took his bid. "I got two dollars from that young man," pointing his finger at Tom. "Who will make it three?" Before Tom knew what had happened the auctioneer sold the basket and a little lady gave him the box and held out her hand for the two dollars.

Tom gave her the two dollars and turned to see a young dark haired gal with big doe eyes smiling at him. Neither of them said anything but Tom followed her to an open bench where she took the box from him and opened it.

"Hope you like chicken and apple pie," she said with a flash of white teeth and a cute smile. She was petite, with long black hair. Her trim figure covered by a calico print dress of red and white. "I'm Val, short for Valance which was my mother's maiden name. What's your name? You're new around here aren't you?"

Val's speech was like pop-corn popping, fast and in spurts. Her magnetic personality put Tom at ease and before either of them had taken their second bite they were acting like old friends.

Tim wasn't so lucky. The girl that fixed the box he purchased was socially shy and timid. Megan was cute enough, but so self-conscious that both felt uncomfortable. It wasn't until Tim reached for another piece of chicken and spilled his punch that both of them relaxed. As it happened they both bent to pick up the cup at the same time and bumped heads. They both laughed and started talking.

CHAPTER FIVE

The morning air was clear and cool. Tim and Tom were saddled up and letting their broncs buck the kinks out. Wade tightened the cinch on his saddle and watched. He was proud of these two young men. They had turned into real good hands, the kind that were loyal to the brand they rode for.

The horses in the corral put the smell of dust in the air as they milled around. Fifty head of the finest horse flesh in Colorado, all green broke and ready to sell. They should bring sixty dollars a head or more, the demand for horses had driven up the price.

With some of that money they could buy some cows and branch out into the cattle business. Right now, all they had was a couple of milk cows. They had plenty of good grazing land and with Tim and Tom to help with the work, they could swing it.

Sweeny joined them, Jake was already mounted on his pony. The five of them would drive the horses to Denver. Sweeny had the buckboard hitched for Penny and Judith. Judith's mother would stay with Chet, Dusty and Sarah while they were gone. The Schroeder's, Judith's parents and brothers had a ranch just a few miles west. They had all come out together on the wagon train from Missouri. It was on this wagon train that Wade and Judith fell in love.

Penny and Judith would lead the way in the buckboard, this way they wouldn't have to eat any dust and the horses would have something to follow.

At first the horses wanted to buck and run, but after a mile or so they settled down. By the time the women got to the main gate and opened it, they followed as if it were a daily occurrence.

Once in Denver, with the horses in one of the corrals, the two boys were anxious to get going. They wanted to get to the barber shop, take a bath and go see the girls they had met at the box-social. Val's father was the local undertaker, and Megan was the daughter of James Miller, a storekeeper.

"We can handle things now, can't we Wade?" Sweeny asked as he closed the gate on the horses.

"Sure."

"You guys can take off. Don't spend all your money in one place." Sweeny smiled as he watched them head for the barbershop.

"Nothing like a pretty gal to turn a young man's head."

"Do you miss chasing the girls?" Judith questioned.

"Sure, don't you miss flirting with the boys?"

"Who said I had stopped?"

Sweeny laughed, gave Wade a little punch on the shoulder and teased, "When you going to learn you can't get the best of her?"

Wade didn't say anything, he just shrugged his shoulders and watched the women and Jake as they made their way toward the shops. He and Sweeny would stay and talk to the horse buyers who were already looking over the horses. There just never seemed to be enough good horse flesh. Between the army, the mining camps, and people going on west, horses were in great demand.

In less than an hour Sweeny and Wade had sold all fifty head. They were happy with their sales and wanted to get to the bank before it closed.

"Even better than I expected," Sweeny said.

Wade nodded as he opened the door to the bank and entered. Neither of them had ever borrowed money before. It had always been either pay cash or do without. But they wanted to get in the cattle business and still have money for operating expenses, so they would have to take out a loan to do that. Right now they only had a couple cows for milk and a steer or two to eat each year. They would like to get about a hundred head of stock cows and several bulls to expand into the cattle business.

"Besides your account here at the bank, what else do you have to back up this note?" The man behind the big walnut desk gazed up at them through thick glasses. His cheeks were clean-shaven, but he wore a mustache and goatee, both clipped neatly. His forehead was broad, nose straight and eyes an expressionless gray.

"We got a herd of horses, two log homes, barns, sleds and each of us have 160 acres of land," Wade replied.

"I'll have to have you sign all of that to back the note." The man shifted his weight in the chair. "Should you fail to make payment, the bank will take over your holdings."

"No need to worry about that, we're not about to let that happen," Sweeny said.

"I'll have the papers drawn up. Stop in the morning," He picked up some papers as if to say they were done.

Didn't even shake hands, Wade thought as he turned to leave. Someday there would be another bank in Denver and he would take his business there. This man made him feel like he was begging, hell wasn't the bank in the business of loaning money. The interest they were paying was more than enough for the bank to make a reasonable profit.

"Well, that wasn't so bad," Sweeny said as the two made their way through the bank.

"If I had another choice I'd take my money out of there and never step foot in the place again," Wade's jaw was set eyes fixed. "I had all I could do to keep from reaching over that desk and jerking him up by his fancy shirt. Who the hell does he think he is anyway?"

"That's just the way of bankers," Sweeny consoled. "At least we got the loan, and can buy us some cows."

Wade didn't reply. He was still hot under the collar, both at himself and the banker. At the banker for acting like God and at himself for letting it get under his skin.

CHAPTER SIX

"We got to do something about Dull-knife and his murdering bunch." There was a crowd of people listening to a Mountain Man.

Wade remember years ago, coming up over a rise he saw a puff of smoke coming from the rocks below, and in a few seconds, another puff. The sound was delayed because of the distance. He pulled his Henry. Riding on, he dropped down in a basin and lost sight of the gun battle.

Rounding a small bluff, he pulled up. In a narrow ravine was a small bunch of Indians. They were pinned down by rifle fire from the rocks to the east. Several appeared to be dead. Two bodies lay outside, they never made it to the protection of the ditch. Looking more carefully Wade couldn't believe his eyes. The Indians were mostly women and children. It wasn't a gun battle, it was all one sided.

Wade didn't know who was in the rocks, but it didn't matter, he leveled his Henry and as fast as he could lever the action, he shot six rounds. He was too far away for good, accurate shooting and his only target was the spots he had seen smoke come from. But it was enough, he saw two men jump to their feet and run to their horses. Big brave men he thought as he rode down to where the Indians were. The sign told the story, the Indians had been fired upon and had made a run for the ditch. Two dead bodies lay on the ground outside the ditch. Inside, there were three more, two women and a boy of maybe twelve. Another boy, a little older, the nearest thing to a warrior in the group, was working over a young girl. She had lost blood that was apparent. She had been shot in the back of the head, behind her ear. Her black hair was matted with blood.

Wade got his canteen and a clean cloth from his saddle bad. Pouring water on the cloth, he handed it to the young brave. He bathed and cleaned the wound, holding the cloth on it to stop the bleeding. The young brave did not appear to have been hit. Another boy, about the same age had been shot in the leg. An older brave, near fifty, had a burn on his arm and another on his thigh. Al older woman was unhurt.

Their ponies lay dead or dying. Those two killers had opened up, hitting whatever they could. These people had never made war on anyone they were doing no harm why would anyone want to do this?

Just then Wade heard riders coming from the north. He looked up to see the Schroeder's. They must have heard the shooting and came to check it out. Wade waved them to come on in and went to meet them.

"Can you get a wagon? We'll take them to my place for now." Wade hardly got the words out when Kemp whirled his horse around and rode back the way he had come.

James and Jokob stayed to help. They cleaned wounds as best they could, wrapped the dead in blankets, took the equipment from the ponies, and shot the ponies that were still alive but too shot up to make it. Kemp returned with the wagon and they loaded the dead and the equipment from the ponies in the front. While they were doing this the old man was repeating something over and over. They had no idea what he was trying to tell them, so they nodded and smiled.

"Get into the wagon," Wade said as he lifted the young girl and placed her in the back on a blanket. The old man was shaking his head and repeating the same thing over and over. Wade motioned for them to get in the wagon, but they didn't seem to want any part of it. Wade picked up one boy and placed him beside the girl, again he motioned for the others to get in. It took some time, but finally they were all loaded. They had five Indians, one hurt bad. She was still unconscious, from the blow of the slug to her head. It had been a glancing blow, had it been a direct hit to the back of her head she would be dead.

Later they saw Music and Sweeny riding toward them. Sweeny had taken the wagon on in and returned with Music.

"Any trouble?" Wade asked.

"No, two riders came into the valley early this morning, but when I let them know I was there they turned and I haven't see hide nor hair of them." Music replied with a shrug.

"We best get on home," Jokob stated. "Take the team and wagon, return it when you can." He motioned for his sons to follow. "I don't want to leave our place unguarded."

The sun was low in the west when they reached the cabin, and it was almost as difficult getting the Indians out of the wagon as it was getting them in it. Wade carried the girl in his cabin and placed her in one of the bunks. Her wound had stopped bleeding but she was still out cold. Her breathing seemed better and she had better color in her face. She wasn't more than seventeen, pretty with full lips and jet black hair. Wade opened her eyes to check for concussion, he had seen this done many times during the war. He knew that a blow to the head could cause serious brain injury. Her large dark eyes appeared to be okay, he wished a doctor was nearer but he knew that many doctors wouldn't walk across the street to treat an Indian.

Sweeny managed to get the Indians to relax and understand they were not prisoners. He used signs best he could, spoke soft and smiled. The older of the boys went to the wagon and started to lift out the dead. Somehow, Sweeny made him realize he would help.

Across the creek on the north, a half-mile from the cabin was a high mound, covered with pine trees. They took the dead to this area and made burial stands. They placed each of the dead on a stand, six to seven feet high. The old brave and woman fixed the dead for burial, using roots and herbs to make a mixture to cover their bodies. Once completed, they sat down near the stream, wrapped in blankets and sang a chant, over and over, all night.

Music took some food and supplies to the Indians, but it was as if they didn't even see him. They continued their chant, repeating over and over the same musical phrase, a rhythmic succession of tones that sounded haunting to the whites.

In the morning the young girl's eyes were open. When she saw Wade. She said something, but the fear and hate in her eyes told Wade it wasn't something he wanted to hear.

"Music, go get the young boy," Wade said gently. The shock of this could be enough to kill her in this weakened condition. Music returned with the young brave, who spoke to her in soft tones. Wade gave him a bowl of soup that he fed to her. She drank some water and was soon back to sleep.

"With some rest, she should be up and around in a few days." Wade said hopefully. The bullet had hit at an angle, making a bad gash behind her ear.

The Indians made a camp by the stream. They cooked their own meals, bringing food to the cabin for the girl. The old woman had picked herbs to make a paste to put on the wound. The girl was better, she was awake more and she ate and drank more.

The third morning, when Wade checked her, she was awake, she smiled at him and softly said, "Thank you."

"Oh, you speak English," Wade said, surprised to hear her speak.

"Yes, a little," she said shyly. "Could I have water?"

"Yes, sure." He went to the bucket and got her some fresh cold water.

She took a deep drink and laid back. Wade was bent low over the bunk. She reached up and touched his necklace.

"Where did you get bear-tooth necklace?"

"Friend. Indian friend gave it to me."

"Has meaning, friend wish you strength of bear. What your friend's name?" She asked in good clear English.

"Spotted Tail. My people were in a spot much like you were, and he helped us. I gave him some things, he gave this to me." Wade held the tooth, thoughtfully, "It was many miles east of here." He said pointing to the east.

Just then, Sweeny gave a yell for Wade to come out on the porch. Fifty or sixty Indians were coming up the valley toward the cabin. They were riding slow. Spread out behind their leader, who was on a pretty paint horse. They wore war-paint, bright yellow and red on their faces. The young brave raced to meet them. He ran a half-mile down the valley to where they stopped, waiting for him. He spoke with the leader, pointing toward the burial-ground, and then to the cabin. The leader gave him a hand and swung him up on his horse behind him. He raised his hand and they rode toward the Indian camp by the stream.

Going back to the girl's bunk, he spoke softly to her, "Looks like some of your friends have come for you."

With Wade's help the girl got up and walked to the door. "That is Dull-Knife, I am to be his," she said filled with admiration. "We were on our way to his camp when attacked."

Dull-Knife, talked to the old brave and woman, mounted and rode toward the cabin. He was tall and lean, a strong looking man. Older than Wade thought he would be, but he was a Cheyenne Chief, and you did not get to be Chief at a young age. He spoke to the girl. He sat his horse with pride and you could see he was at home on its back. The girl turned to Wade.

She began hesitantly, "Dull-Knife want to know if you want me?"

Wade did not know what to say, he was shocked by the question. If he said no, Dull-Knife could take it as an insult. If he said yes, he may have himself a woman he hardly knew. Cursing silently, Wade hoped what he was about to say was what the Indian wanted to hear.

"I would be proud to have such a prize, but you belong to Dull-Knife, with him you should be." He had much to learn of the Indian and their ways. He did know that they were a proud people.

The girl told Dull-Knife what Wade had said. The Indian smiled and called to one of his braves. The brave rode to the cabin leading a pony for the girl.

"Are you strong enough to ride?"

"Yes, I will be fine. It is not far." She looked up into Wade's eyes and said joyously. "Thant you." The brave helped her to mount.

Dull-Knife swept his arm in a wide circle, saying a few words to the girl.

"Dull-Knife says this valley is special, that he and his tribe will protect it and you from any harm." With that they turned and rode at a walk down the valley. Wade knew they had made a friend.

Wade, came back to the here and now.

"You say it was Dull-Knife?" Someone yelled from the crowd.

"Yes, Dull-Knife and that band of killers. Last week he hit a mining camp, killed everyone. Early this week he hit a supply wagon headed for Fort Morgan." At the mention of their Indian friend's name, Wade and Sweeny both paid special attention.

"That's twenty or more people Dull-Knife and his band of cut-throats have killed in the last two weeks." The man had an audience and he wasn't going to pass up his chance to give them an ear full.

"Has anyone seen Dull-Knife?" Wade asked.

"How can they, he never leaves anyone alive, but the soldiers traced him to just north of Denver, before he gave them the slip." The man's eyes shot fire at Wade for even asking such a stupid question.

"If no one has seen him, how do they know it was Dull-Knife?" Wade started to walk on past.

"You calling me a liar?" He drew back his arm to take a swing and reached for his knife with his other hand. Sweeny following Wade, caught the man's wrist and held it in his vice-like grip. At the same time, Wade's hand cleared his Colt. Before the man knew what had happened, he was looking at the business end of Wade's Colt and his arm was being held by the strongest grip he had ever felt.

"No, we didn't say you lied. I just asked a question." Wade's voice was soft and calm, but his eyes told the man he could get shot if he pushed this thing too far. "If no one has seen him, or any Indian, how do we know it was Dull-Knife?" Wade repeated.

The mountain man had never seen a gun jump into a man's hand any faster and if this red-head was as tough as his grip, he would just as soon fight a bear.

Wade released the hammer on his Colt, dropping it back into his holster. Smiling he said, "Seems to me, Dull-Knife could be getting credit for things he's not doing."

"Well….sure nuff, but Dull-Knife's the only Red Skin that has been seen 'round these parts." His voice was not so sure, not so boastful or threatening. Sweeny eased his grip on the man's wrist. It was over for now, even this tough old mountain man knew when to back off.

"Could be white men, I've seen some pretty low and worthless white's in this area." The crowd was breaking up, going their way.

Wade didn't give him a chance to say anything else, he turned and walked toward the bar. The street returned to normal, with the threat ended, everyone had better things to do.

They ran into Music, a man that came out from St. Joe with them.

"Well. George Washing…." Music interrupted him, "No, just Music, you hung that handle on me and how that's all I go by. Even Sadie calls me Music." He walked with a slight limp, a souvenir of the Civil War. Wade had nicknamed him Music because he could make music out of anything from his banjo to a set of spoons.

"We were just thinking of looking you up, we just got into town," Sweeny shook his hand.

"How's Sadie?"

"Great, pregnant and getting more that way every day," Music said with a smile from ear to ear.

"What? Let me buy you a beer." Wade said as they walked up on the boardwalk and into the bar.

They were getting caught up on the news of their families when the mountain man interrupted. He had a little whiskey in him and had some of his courage back.

"First you defend the Indians and now ya drink with a nigger!" He was letting his anger and prejudice get in the way of his common sense.

He was about to say something else when he caught Sweeny's big fist, square in the mouth. Blood sprang from his split lips as his head snapped back. But he took the blow and came right at Sweeny, swinging with lefts and rights. Sweeny took a glancing blow to the head and countered with a left to his mid-section. The two giants stood toe to toe and slugged. Both had the power to put the average man down and out. Sweeny was the best at blocking and slipping the punches. It soon paid off, the mountain man was arm weary and when Sweeny saw the opening, he nailed him dead on the chin. The man's eyes rolled back into his head from the force of the blow. He was out cold before he hit the sawdust floor.

Nothing had been broken so things went on as usual. They had several fights a day, and unless someone was killed or something got broken, no one worried about it. Two guys grabbed the mountain man by his heels and drug him out the back door. He would wake up in the alley.

Sweeny, didn't look too bad, he had caught a blow high on his right eye, and could have a black eye in the morning but that was about it.

"Haven't been in a good barroom brawl in years." Sweeny was winded and beads of sweat showed on his forehead but the smile on his face showed he had enjoyed himself.

"Let me buy you a beer," Music said. "Guess I was the cause of it," he added in his slow drawl.

"No, we had words earlier, but I could use another beer."

"What's Penny going to say, you getting into a fight?" Wade asked with a smile.

"She won't like it, but when she finds out what he said, she could just go looking for him herself."

They enjoyed another beer, told Music the news and went to find their families.

"Yes, we heard stories of Dull-Knife too. I wanted so much to say they were not true, but I bite my lip and said nothing." Penny touched the swelling above Sweeny's eye and smiling added, "Boys will be boys."

In 1866 Dull-Knife had joined Red Cloud and the Oglala Sioux in ambushing U.S. soldiers under Captain William Fitterman traveling the Bozeman Trail to reach the Montana gold fields. It was called a massacre, but when the Cavalry would attack an Indian village and kill women and children it was called a great frontier victory.

CHAPTER SEVEN

Everything in the valley was fine when they got back from Denver with supplies and a loan to buy some cattle. Kemp had checked on Mrs. Schroeder daily and stayed with her one night, Jokob had come and also stayed a night. He got to enjoy Chet and Sarah. Judith had not told them of the new grandchild but she would have to soon as she was starting to show signs.

Wade and Sweeny had made arrangements for some cows and a few bulls to be delivered later in the week. The cows would drop calves next spring. They would have to cut more hay to feed them during the hard Colorado winter. With the help of Tom and Tim the job would be easier and go faster.

The cattle buyer had to deliver cattle to Fort Morgan, so he would drop their cows off on his way to Fort Morgan. They were now in the cattle business, horses were still worth more than cattle so they would continue to raise and catch wild horses to break for the army.

Wade had his second cup of coffee and was out on the porch watching the sun come up in the east when he noticed a little dust in the air. Watching it develop into a group of Indians coming into the valley. Moving slowly they made their way toward his cabin. After a time he made out the leader to be Dull-Knife, he looked as if he had been treated harshly, and he and his people looked to be weathered and worn. Once a powerful tribe, he and his band had been reduced to not much more than women and children. He had sent most of the warriors north to Montana to hunt. While they were gone the U. S. Cavalry hit their village. He had advanced warning so he took the women and children to hide in the rocks.

Before the end of the Civil War the Crow were the traditional enemy of the Cheyenne, now the Crow scouts helped the Cavalry find and fight the Cheyenne. With his warriors gone, he had to find a place to hide, he hated even the sound of the word, but it was either that, be shot, or confined to a reservation.

Dull-Knife was riding the black and white pinto with the Eagle Brand on its hip, the one Wade had given him. Like his rider the pinto looked in need of a place to rest and gain back some strength.

The eagle was known as the "Chief of all Birds" and the Cheyenne regarded it as the emblem of strength and courage. They needed strength and courage now more than ever before.

Wade put his coffee cup on the porch rail and stepped down to walk and meet the Indians. Behind him, standing in the open door of the cabin was Judith.

From another cabin, several hundred yards back in the valley, Sweeny came out to see why the dog was barking. He and Jake walked toward Wade and the Indians.

"Chief Dull-Knife, welcome to our home," Wade could not believe his eyes, these people were in bad shape. Many were walking, and what horses they had were in sorry shape.

Dull Knife dismounted and the young girl that Wade had saved years before stepped forward, Morning Star was the third wife of Dull-Knife. The girl told them of the braves going north to hunt and that the soldiers had come to their village destroying the contents, burning and driving off the horses that they had not managed to hide. She told them that they had come here to hide until their men returned from the hunt.

"You understand that we cannot fight the Cavalry for you, but we can give you a place where I think you will be safe." The girl translated this to Dull-Knife. The Indian Chief nodded his head, and speaking to the girl he motioned for his people to follow him.

"Dull-Knife thanks you." She looked much older than the last time he saw her.

It wasn't long and the small band went into the barn and out the back and into the box canyon. The canyon was large and the sides were sheer rock, a couple hundred feet high, a spring supplied water and the game was plentiful.

They fixed a camp by the spring and soon had a fire going. Sweeny and Jake gave them some venison and bread. They were a sorry looking bunch, but they were proud and they had survived bone-chilling blizzards, starvation, the white man's diseases, and they would survive this too.

Wade and Sweeny opened one of the corrals and drove a small herd of horses to the gate and back, hoping to cover any sign of the Indians.

"Did you ever see such a sight," Judith said, "Those poor people, I don't know how they made it this far."

"They will be alright in the canyon. They have everything they need there." He was thinking about what he would tell the troops when they came and they were sure to come.

"The cattle should be here in the morning that will cover all the tracks. I hope the cattle get here before the troops."

"You can't turn them over to the Army," Judith said, almost as a question

"I know, but I can't go against my country either." He thought now about the Civil War and the agony of defeat he and the South had suffered. He remembered all too well his feeling when he returned to the plantation in Tennessee and found it burned to the ground. The emptiness as he stood over the graves of his parents. How was this any different? In the blink of an eye everything can change. Now he had Judith, Chet and little Sarah and soon they would have another child. He knew that if they were found harboring Indians he would be in big trouble. But he also knew that if it had not been for Indians, Spotted Tail and Dull-Knife he would not have all this. He could not turn his back on Dull-Knife, not at a time like this.

Sweeny and Penny entered the cabin, "We need to talk." Sweeny said. They were good friends, Wade had joined Penny and her son Jake in Tennessee. Traveled with them until they meet Judith and her family.

In St. Joe Sweeny joined them for the trip to Colorado. Together they had built Eagle Valley.

"We owe a great deal to these people." Sweeny took a cup of coffee from Judith.

"I know, we were just talking about it before you walked in," Wade took a sip of coffee and went on. "Judith feels we must do all we can for Dull-knife and his people."

"If it weren't for them, who knows, maybe we wouldn't even be married." Penny put her hand on Sweeny's arm.

"I don't worry about anyone finding them in the canyon. Building the barn in front of the entrance, and with hay piled in front of the door, a soldier could walk in the barn and never guess it was there."

"The canyon is not a great deal better than a reservation."

"True, but no one put them in there and they can leave whenever they want, the Cavalry has no reason to suspect that we would hide them," Judith knew it could be trouble for them but she felt for these people.

"That's true, but there's no way out of that canyon, and if later on they find them leaving the valley they will know."

"That's the chance we will have to take. That is one of those bridges we will cross when we come to it," Judith gave him a punch on the shoulder and smiled.

They visited and drank another pot of coffee. They all agree that for the time being, all they could do was to hope and pray the Army didn't find them or see them when they were ready to leave. The Indians would be no trouble, they could live off the land. The canyon was full of deer and other game. The deer would provide them with food, clothing, and shelter.

Early the next morning, Wade went into the hidden canyon. He was surprised to see that everyone was up and doing something. Many were fixing their hair. The Indian's hair was of great importance to them. They believed that their hair was in some way connected with the length of life. The men had their hair in two long braids and wrapped in beaver skin, allowing it to hang down on their chests. The women wore their hair in a single braid.

Going to where Dull-Knife was, Wade noticed just how badly battered and bruised they were. It would be days, even weeks before they could move on again. Their horses were in worse shape if that were possible. Their bridles, thongs that were looped around the horses' lower jaws, were in a pile by the fire. All the horses had a neck rope dragging so they would be easy to catch.

Using Morning Star as an interpreter, Wade spoke to Dull-Knife. He felt that Dull-Knife understood a great deal more than he let on and Wade would not be surprised if he could speak the white man's language too. He asked if there was anything that they needed, when he was assured there wasn't he returned to his home.

He found Chet up eating his breakfast and Sarah in the high chair.

They were both special to him. Only Judith was more important. He would give his life for them.

"How are they doing? They getting along okay?

"They're fine. All fixing their hair, but they are going to need some time before they will be ready to leave, and they don't know when the hunting party will return."

"And your little Indian maid, how's she?"

"She's just fine, and don't get too uppity or I just may take Dull-Knife up on his offer to give her to me."

"Oh you will, will you? Hear that kids? Your father is ready to trade me off already."

Wade should have known better, saying something smart to Judith was like waving a red flag at a bull. He never could best her at the word game. Drinking his coffee he remembered back to the day on the wagon train, he told her that it worried him her riding alone and she told him that she thought he only cared about older women.

The barking of the dog told him somebody was coming. He looked out the window to see the cattle coming into the valley. He and Sweeny, saddled up and went to meet them. They made the count and Wade signed the tally slip. The man would take it to the bank for his money. One hundred head at forty dollars came to four thousand dollars.

Later that same day, Wade saw a troop of soldiers riding down toward the cabin. They were still at least two miles away, so he yelled to Jake to warn the Indians.

Wade could not look at a troop of Union Cavalry without remembering the Civil War. But as far as he was concerned, Johnny Reb and Billy Yank had ended their quarrel. It was over, the North had won. He often wondered if things would be different had the South have won.

"Good morning Captain. What can I do for you?" The officer in charge was young, Wade had not seen him before and he sold horses at both Fort Logan and Fort Morgan.

"Looking for a bunch of Indians. Lost their track just outside the entrance to your valley."

"Saw a bunch yesterday, mostly women and children, they were heading east. But they didn't look very dangerous."

"Their Leader is Dull-Knife," the Captain answered. "And he can take anything and make it into a fighting force."

Sweeny and Jake joined them and both women came to the doors of their cabins to watch what was going on.

"Won't you step down and have something to eat with us, isn't often we get visitors?

"No, we have to be moving. So many horse and cattle tracks, we thought maybe they came this way, but I can see that it is a box canyon so guess we will head east and see if we can pick-up any sign." The young officer raised his hand and signaled his men to follow.

They watched as the troop rode at a trot back toward the main gate. Well that hadn't been so bad, there was no reason to suspect them of hiding the Indians.

"Whew. I wouldn't make a very good crook, my heart was in my throat all the time," Jake said.

"Mine too Jake, nobody likes to lie, but in this case I think it was for the best." Wade put his arm around Jake and they walked away.

CHAPTER EIGHT

The Indians were truly great horsemen. Wade and Sweeny had rounded up some wild mustangs so they would have enough horses when it was time to leave. They put them in the canyon and Dull-Knife and what braves he had, were breaking them.

They broke their horses in a way Wade had never seen. Using a blanket they would almost hypnotize the horse. They mounted from the right side, instead of the left as did the horsemen Wade knew. The mounting on the left was carried down from the old days when it was custom to wear a sword on the left side. The Indians were not bound by any such custom and mounted in the way that seemed natural.

Dull-Knife's horsemanship was truly excellent. He could slip to the side of a speeding pony and shoot from beneath the animal's neck. He rode bareback or with only a pad of animal skins. Guiding his horse with pressure of his legs. They decorated their ponies with paint and cloth tied to manes and tails. Dull-Knife favored the flashy pinto that Wade had given him with the Eagle brand on its hip, he thought the horse had magical powers. Wade and Sweeny learned much from watching the Indians work. They also learned something else too. There was another way out of the hidden canyon. One of the Indians had found it. It had been hidden by a large pine tree. It was narrow and steep, difficult to ascend but the deer used it and a horse could make it. It came out on the bluffs and from there you could ride north or west with ease.

Dull-Knife had sent one of the braves to go and find the hunting party, let them know what had happened and where they were. They had to get back together for strength. Dull-Knife's first son, Hump Bull was with the hunting party. Morning Star was his third wife, each wife had given him descendants to carry on his honorable descent.

The Indians had taken thin strips of meat, dried it on racks in the sun and made jerky. They had made bows and arrows, gathered seeds, nuts, roots, and parts of plants. They were getting ready to leave, they were much stronger, and their horses were in excellent shape. Dull- Knife told Wade of the land to the north where he was born, the Rose Bud River, where there was good hunting and fishing. The winters there were very difficult, for that reason there were not many white men in the area. This is where he would lead his people. He would meet up with the hunting party and he would once again have a strong band that could protect itself.

They were all rather sad to see them packing, making ready to leave. They had learned a great deal from each other, most important that the white man and the red man could live together in peace.

Dull-Knife led the way up the steep trail and out of the canyon that had been their hiding place.

"Good Luck," Wade said as he waved to the Indians high on the canyon wall. They were much too far to hear but the wave of the hand was a sign they could see and understand. Dull-Knife stopped his pinto pony and waved to the group watching from far below. He led his band to the north, dropping out of sight in minutes.

It wasn't until many years later that they learned what happened to Dull-Knife. He was captured and placed on a reservation in Indian Territory, which is now Oklahoma. But with no buffalo to hunt and his people near starvation, in 1878 he led his band north. They had to fight their way across Kansas, and were finally captured and confined to Fort Robinson in Nebraska. But instead of surrendering all their arms, they took them apart and concealed them under blankets. The children wore bracelets and necklaces of hammers, firing pins, and other gun parts.

One bitter night in January, 1879 they made yet another break for freedom with their reassembled guns. A great many women and children were shot, Dull-Knife escaped.

Dull-Knife died in 1883, and was buried on a high butte near the valley of the Rosebud River. His grave overlooking the country he so wanted to share with his band of people.

CHAPTER NINE

Each Sunday they would all gather at Schroeder's place to worship. Jokob would preach, they would have a big meal, sing and thank their Lord for their many blessings. This Sunday, Music, Sadie, and their young son joined the group.

It was back at the Wilbur's that evening that Chet teased Music to sing.

His first request was the Preacher and the Bear. When Music would get to the chorus, Chet knew the words and he would join in.

Chorus:

"Oh Lord, you delivered Daniel from the bottom of the Lion's den

You delivered Joanna, from the belly of the whale and then,

The Hebrew children from the fiery furnace so the good books do declare.

Oh Lord, if you can't help me, for God's sake don't help that bear."

Music would add his own little extra to the song.

"Now Lord it may not look like much from where you sit up there, but the hardest job you ever gave me was to baptize that there grizzly bear."

They would sing the chorus again and each time Chet would get a little louder. Wade had to smile at his boy and Judith just shook her head.

"Sing it again Music."

"You just leave Music be, you have pestered him to sing enough." But Judith had to admit that she enjoyed it almost as much as Chet.

*Author Joe Arzonia 1881, Arthur Collins, was the first to record the song, in 1905 – I first heard it sung by my good friend Rex Browning, 1960

CHAPTER TEN

They were in Fort Morgan selling horses to the army, Wade, Judith, Penny, Sweeny, Tom and Tim. The kids had stayed back in the valley with Judith's mother. Penny and Judith wanted to shop in the commissary. They promised the children they would bring them something.

Wade and Sweeny were just coming out of the Paymaster's office with the pay slip for the horses. This would make a nice payment on their loan at the Denver bank.

They noticed a troop of Cavalry coming back to Fort Morgan. The whole camp was coming out to greet them, to see if they had suffered any loss of life on this latest patrol. The wives of the officers and enlisted men gathered to welcome their men.

The women on post were a clannish, gossipy, bunch divided by jealousy but united the moment their men went to battle. Now they watched their men return with what looked like a white women. She wore U.S. Cavalry breeches, covered with either a long deerskin shirt or a short dress. The fringe cut in the bottom came to just above her knees. Even dressed like this she was a lovely woman.

To those watching, she had beauty on the outside, but was dirty, ugly, on the inside. She should be dead. To survive was to mean she had given in to the demands. On her back she carried the proof. In a cradleboard, wrapped is soft skins, was a baby. From a hoop over his head dangled bright and jingling toys. These, rather than the crowd held his attention.

She was rigid on the horse, accepting neither sympathy or disapproval from the judges that lined the compound. But she couldn't help but hear some of the crude jokes or comments. She had learned from her father, long ago to take the hand fate dealt and play it the best she could. That is what she had done.

"Just two more for the government to care for." A short, plump woman was talking. "What will they do with her and her baby?"

"Be another camp follower. A whore to take the soldier's money on payday."

"Bess. You make sure John gets her out of camp." All eyes turned to the wife of John Chivington, the commander of Fort Morgan.

They tolerated the prostitutes from the alley. Those were fat, ugly, toothless harlots that were not a threat to their womanhood. They had seen the way the men drank in the beauty of this woman as if she were an intoxicating alcohol. This woman was young, and even the hard work and life as an Indian had not dimmed her beauty.

"Look at her, wearing clothes from some poor dead soldier. She most likely has his scalp tied to her belt." The woman spit in the dust. "She should have died with all the other Indians." This was the sentiment of most of the white people. Her future and the future of her baby was not bright, to say the least.

Wade and Sweeny joined the ladies in the commissary. They too wanted to look around and see if there wasn't something that they just couldn't live without.

"What did you make of all the excitement," Wade asked Judith.

"The poor woman, to survive all she had to endure, only to receive this welcome. That's not right."

"How long have you been a captive?" Lieutenant Colonel Chivington, sat behind a big oak desk, his eyes scanning the woman standing before him.

He had led his men to the camp of the Cheyenne, the Crow scouts had done their job well. He led his troops to a summit where his men set up two howitzers and began to shell the camp. First with artillery fire and then with rifles. Neither she nor her baby had suffered a scratch, for this she thanked the Great Spirit.

"Little more than a year," she replied.

"How did this come about?" The commander asked.

"Provisions were scarce in the mining camps, flour sold for $45 a sack. A wagon or two and a man could have the ranch of his dreams." She paused and looked at a chair.

"Excuse me, please have a chair, make yourself comfortable."

"Thank you." She took the baby from her back and held him in front as she sat down. "My father, Sam Parker, took a small wagon train of provisions through Indian Territory. Had he made it, he would have been a rich man. We were only twenty-five miles from the mining camp when we were attacked." Again she paused and took a deer skin and placed it over her baby. She reached in under the skin to allow her baby to suck nourishment.

"This Big Bear, did he slaughter all the others on the wagon train?" He hoped and prayed for her to finish feeding her baby before someone came in or she departed.

"Big Bear said only my beauty saved me from the destiny of the others," she replied.

"You sound as if Big Bear were a friend."

"He took me for his own. He is the father of my boy."

"Doesn't the loss of your family and now the loss of Big Bear distress you?"

"I do what I must." Dressed in a mixture of Indian and white man's clothing she also seemed to have a mixture of their strength.

"I do not know what to do with or for you," the officer looked perplexed. "Do you have any family?"

"No. Both my white and my Indian family have been killed." She always tried to look at a situation from the other person's point of view. That was how she learned the game of poker from her father and that was the way she played the game of life. Now she struggled to understand what he might be thinking, what were his aces, what was his bluff's, and did either of them have a pat hand?

What are your options?" She asked.

"Well. I could." He paused to think. "I could keep you here, give you quarters until you have a place to go or a job to support yourself." His hand made a circular motion on the top of his desk. "I could send you to St. Louis, turn you over to command." Again the circular motion. "I could just turn you loose, detach myself from you." This time his hand went to his face, he rubbed his chin and nose before going on. "I could send your baby to the reservation, but only Indians can go there, so…."

"That is not one of your options!" She interrupted.

"What?"

"No one will separate us." She said looking down at her baby.

"What is his name?"

"Indian boys are not given a name until they earn one by doing some worthy deed. Until that time, they are called by some nickname. His father called his Luta."

"Luta, what does this mean?"

"Scarlet, he was very red when born." She smiled down at the baby still working on his lunch.

"And your name, Miss Parker, what is your name?"

"I was Patty Ann Parker, now I am Tawny."

"Surely you do not plan to keep your Indian name and ways?" His eyes searched her face for a trace of comprehension.

"When the Indian wins a battle, it is called a massacre, when the Cavalry commits a massacre it is called a battlefield victory. I am sorry, but yes, I do want to keep some of the Indian ways of living." For a moment neither spoke. They both looked into each other's eyes, attempting to read what they could.

"What Indian ways would you wish to keep?"

"To burn or bury all rubbish. Not to destroy the beauty of the land. Not to kill more game than your people need, or pick more berries than they will eat, or gather more fuel than they can burn. Be kind to the weak, honor the old, and always give your guest the place of honor in your lodge, and never sit while he is standing."

Remembering, the commander's face became red. She went on, "The Indian can see a humorous side to nearly every problem, and I don't want to lose that and many other things I learned this past year." She paused to reach under the deer skin and replace her breast and put her baby up on her shoulder. As she patted his back she went on. "That isn't to say I want to go on working like an Indian woman. A year of that is enough to last me a life time."

"What would you have me do?" His question was an honest one, he wanted to do as she wished.

"Allow me to rest here at the fort a day or two." She got to her feet and turned to leave. Stopping at the door she turned and added. "I will let you know what I wish to do and where I wish to go."

"Fine." He jumped to his feet, putting both hands on his desk he leaned forward. "Plan to have dinner with my family tonight. I know my wife will want to visit with you."

She nodded, but she also remembered some of the remarks she heard from the good women of Fort Morgan. It could be that the commander did not know his wife as well as he thought.

Most women with her beauty and talents could go to any frontier town, attend church, and pick out her man, get married and be a wife and mother. But as long as she had Luta, her past would also be with her. As long as she had Luta, she wouldn't be welcome in most homes and in many churches. Hatred for the Red Man was at a boiling point and an Indian lover was even lower in the eyes of many on the frontier.

CHAPTER ELEVEN

"What did you bring us?" Chet was running to meet the buckboard as Penny and Judith approached the cabin. Judith's mother was holding Sarah on the porch.

"Just hold your horses, until we get inside," Judith said as the team stopped at the hitch rail.

Once in the cabin, Judith gave Chet the chalk board and chalk first. She showed him how he could draw or write on it and wipe it off. He took it to the table and was drawing on it. She gave Sarah the doll. It was wood, about 10 inches tall, the doll maker had done a nice job painting the hair and face. Judith had never had a doll with a face as a young girl. Amish dolls were faceless. She hoped that this would not offend her parents, who still held to many of the Amish ways.

The doll had a skirt with a bustle and train. It also had a red cape and a red bonnet. Sarah held it as if it were made of gold. Judith smiled at the joy she saw on Sarah's face. Going to the table, she handed Chet a ball, about the size of a small babies head and made of canvas.

"Now I don't want you throwing it in the cabin, it's an outdoor toy."

Chet grabbed it and the first thing he did was toss it up in the air and catch it. Looking at his mother and seeing the look on her face, he started for the door.

After supper, Judith showed Chet the Jacob's ladder. It was six solid wood segments attached with colorful cloth ribbon. It was a simple toy, with a very illusive action. Along with the toy she told him the story of Jacob's ladder from the Old Testament. He went to bed holding his ball and Sarah holding her doll.

She and Wade sat at the table, drinking coffee and talking about the day's activities. Wade was happy with the sale of the horses.

"What do you think about the woman, the troopers brought in." he asked Judith.

"What did you think about her?"

Wade knew there was no way to answer that without getting into trouble. He also knew that Judith loved to make him squirm, he was no match for her when it came to word games. Even now she had this, I got you smile on her face.

"I felt sorry for her being paraded in front of the whole fort like she was an animal in the zoo."

Judith nodded. "I am sure she has a story, one that none of us would like to live. I wonder what will become of her and her baby."

"I don't know," he paused, "but I don't think a person's value decreases based on others being unable to see the worth."

"Just like the Indians?" Judith asked.

Wade nodded. He had seen so many good things about the Indians in the short time they were in the canyon. He felt the tooth, he wore around his neck, remembering how Spotted Tail and his band had come to their rescue. True, they were after the men because of what they had done to their camp, their women and children. They did scalp them and it looked like a massacre, but they could have done the same to the wagon train and they didn't.

"I hope she finds someone that sees her value." He said.

"The happiest I've ever felt was the moment when I realized you loved me too." She took his hand and looked up into his eyes.

"Darn, I wish I would have thought to say that." Wade led her to their bed.

The next morning, Sarah came to breakfast holding her doll. Little girls become attached to their dolls and share with them their deepest wishes, sorrows, and joys.

Wade came in from doing chores. He had brushed Eagle and carried the smell with him.

"No one will ever understand my love for 'horse smell' or the peace it brings to me," Judith said as she gave Wade a cup of coffee and his breakfast. "Are you and Sweeny riding in to Denver this morning?"

"Yes, we want to make the payment to the bank. It will cut the interest some and give us both some peace of mind." Wade did not look forward to going in the bank. He did not like the man they dealt with getting the loan, and he did not like himself for feeling that way.

With Wade on Eagle and Sweeny riding a big reddish-brown bay mare the two ranchers headed toward Denver. The only reason they had to go was to make the bank payment, so it would be a quick trip. They would be back before sun down.

Once inside the bank, they went to the wrought iron window. The teller was busy counting money. Once finished he looked up. "May I help you gentleman? He asked. It was not the same man, he had a smile on his face and seemed truly happy to see them.

"Want to make a payment on our loan, can you take care of that for us?" Sweeny said.

"Sure, let me get the loan papers, what's the name on them?"

"Jim McSweeny and Wade Wilbur," Wade said with a touch of pride.

"Here it is, your note is four thousand, what would you like to pay on it today?"

"We have a draft from the Army paymaster at Fort Morgan, its four hundred dollars." Wade replied.

"Okay." He took the slip and wrote out a receipt for them. "That leaves a balance of thirty-six hundred plus interest," he informed them. "Is there anything else I can help you with today?"

"No, thanks, that will be all," Wade said and they turned to walk out of the bank. "It is funny how one man can make such a difference. I feel so much better today, and think of the bank so different." Sweeny nodded, and he couldn't help but smile, remembering how upset Wade had been when they got the loan.

"Guess we could get a beer to cut the dust before he head back to the valley," Wade said.

"Sounds good to me." They mounted and rode toward the bar. Going toward the bar they noticed a sign they had not seen in the past.

"Chief of Police" was printed in large letters on the front of a false fronted building. You could tell it was new, most of the signs showed a little wear from the sun and winter cold. Denver was growing daily and with the growth, came more crime. The city council voted to add a new position, "Chief of Police" and gave him a police force.

In the bar all the talk was of the new law officers, how they dressed, how they walked around town, in and out of the bars. They had taken drunks to jail, were even in the "Cribs" on Market Street.

"The expensive prostitutes on upper Market Street cost five dollars, they don't seem to bother them, but who can afford five dollars a poke?" The man looked to be a storekeeper or merchant of some type. "I only paid six dollars for this here new pocket watch, and they want five bucks a poke?" He held up his watch and checked the time.

Wade and Sweeny finished their beers and turned to leave. They had a long ride and wanted to get home before dark.

It was dark thirty when they rode in. Both cabins had a light in them. They hoped the women had saved them something to eat, it had been a long time since they ate breakfast. The Harper boys came out and asked if they wanted them to take care of their horses.

"Thanks, appreciate you doing this." They wanted to get in to see their wives and kids as soon as possible.

"What did ya bring me?" Chet asked as his dad walked into the cabin.

"Nothing. Didn't take time to do anything but go to the bank. Besides you got more than most yesterday." Sarah didn't care she just wanted her daddy to take her and hold her.

CHAPTER TWELVE

Kemp and his mother were on their way to Fort Morgan. Judith had told them of all the good buys she had seen in the Fort Commissary and they wanted to take advantage of some of them. It was easier than going to Denver.

Sarah liked to go with Kemp for supplies. She didn't get a chance to talk with him one on one very much. He was her oldest, and he worked so hard for the family. He had never had a girlfriend, or even a male friend other than Wade and Sweeny who he meet in Missouri and came to Colorado with on the wagon train. They both had families now and Kemp was still living with his parents.

"Do you ever wish for more?" They were Amish but had broken away from the strict order before they came west. They still wore all black but did not speak or follow the strict ways of the church.

"What do you mean?"

"Do you ever wish that you had a place of your own, a family?"

"Yes, I do think of it some. We have been so busy building, that I have not had the time to worry about it that much." Kemp and his father both smoked, none of the family used 'thee and 'thou' in their speech, but they still held to many of the Amish ways.

In the Fort Commissary, Sarah had her list of the things they needed. Kemp was just wandering around looking at all the different things they had for sale.

"The dirty bitch, she looks like she enjoyed every minute she was with those savages." Kemp snapped his head in the direction of the woman making the comment. He saw two women staring at the woman coming into the store. She had a baby in her arms, wearing a cotton dress, she was very attractive. Her oval face and natural beauty was accented by her big doe eyes. Even this plain cotton dress could not hide her supple body.

Kemp wondered at the comment of the woman. How could she say something so disrespectful? It had not been a casual comment, there was hate in her words. Kemp watched as the woman walked up to what appeared to be the man in charge, she spoke to him and he shook his head in a negative manner.

The Commanding Officer's wife functioned as many things, post hostess, moral standard bearer and often as "den-mother". She often had a sympathetic ear and of course had great influence. In order for a post to be designated a fort, a contingent of troops had to be permanently assigned to it. When this happened some of the officers and enlisted men's wives and children were with them at the fort.

It was like a small town and often the officer's households included female servants, governesses, housekeepers, maids, and cooks. The military also employed laundresses, nurses, as well as a school teacher. Patty Ann Parker, Tawny, had not been able to obtain any type of employment.

Once a year the mountain men came down with their furs. They would drink, fight, tell lies to each other and trade their furs for supplies and whiskey. Wagon trains sent by companies from the east arrive with these necessities and depart with tons of beaver hides. This event had taken place just a week ago, and although Tawny had been made many offers. None of them was anything she was interested in.

Forts were usually laid out with a central parade ground. Officer quarters along one side and enlisted men's barracks on the other. Commissary, hospital, bakery and laundry along one side and the stables along the other. Fort Morgan was laid out like this.

Kemp watched as she walked out not seeming to know which way to turn or go. She was standing by their buckboard when he walked out.

"Hi. You live here at the fort?"

She looked up at him all dressed in black, different than anyone she had seen around the fort. At first she thought he was just another man about to make an improper proposition. But after taking the time to read his eyes and his face, she felt it had been just a question to start a conversation.

"No, I don't live here, the troopers brought me here. I have been trying to find a job and a place to live."

"Not having any luck? I would think there would be lots of jobs around the fort."

"There are but none for me."

"What did you do back east?"

"The last job I had was as a school teacher." The bundle in her arms was wiggling and starting to make a noise. Kemp watched as a head appeared, a stock of black hair, and dark eyes that were bright and seemed to have a smile in them looked up at him. The baby was not very old, six months at the most, but it already had a personality.

"Little boy?"

"Yes, this is Luta."

"You can't find a job because of the small baby?"

"Yes, in a way." She went on to tell him her story. How because of Luta she was not welcome in the fort. How the wives of the officers and enlisted men did not want her around. That she feared they would take Luta away from her and send him to a reservation.

"Do you have any family?"

"No, my white family were killed by the Cherokee and my Indian family killed by the troopers. It is just Luta and me."

"I have to go help my mother with the supplies, why don't you have a seat in the buckboard, make yourself comfortable." Without waiting for her to reply, he took her arm and helped her up to the spring seat.

CHAPTER THIRTEEN

They had turned one of the out buildings into a school and a place for Luta and his mother to live until they could build a real school. Jobok had wanted a church too, so now they thought about combining them into one building. Being that all the young children were at the east end of the valley that would be where they would build.

Jake was the only one old enough for real school, but Chet and Dusty were almost school age, and both were eager to learn. Jake had never been to a school, Penny had always schooled him. Even little Sarah would sit in from time to time.

Miss Parker taught more than just how to read and cipher, she also taught many of the things she learned living with the Indians. Ways to enjoy the beauty of the land. Not to waste, to be kind to the weak and to honor the elderly. She taught them to be thankful for their many blessings and to share.

She taught them history, about the founding of America, about the Civil War and the Colorado Territory. How in 1861 Congress chose as the name for the territory, Colorado. Colorado is of Spanish origin meaning "Colored Red" because of the red sand stone. The slogan, "Pikes Peak or Bust" was written on prairie schooners after John Gregory discovered gold near Central City in 1859.

They took walks to study the animals, wolves, bears, deer, jackrabbits, wild horses, along with the rattlesnakes all native to the valley. The bald Eagles and Sandhill Cranes. She taught them to enjoy and appreciate nature. Also to understand that many by nature would fight to protect their territory, and that to some, humans were food.

Kemp seemed to be around often, watching them on the field trips, or stopping in at school to see if anyone needed anything. They didn't have many books, they had the old McGuffey reader that Jake and Penny had in Tennessee, and a Free Dictionary that Kemp had, along with two different versions of the Bible. All of the men would stop in from time to time and tell a story. Wade told them of the Civil War, leaving out many of the things that they were not old enough to understand. Sweeny told them of Ireland, of why many of the Irish wanted to come to America. Kemp told them about the Amish, and being a good reader, he would read to them from one of the bibles.

They learned to make paint by crushing plants, yellow from the mustard plant, red from berries or from the red sand stone, white from milkweed pods, and black from the soot of a camp fire. With these they learned to paint pictures. Kemp showed them how to use hair from the mane or tail of a horse to make a paint brush.

They learned about the ranch, how to care for the horses and cattle. How to prepare for the cold Colorado winter and the many different ways the animals used to cope with the ice and snow of winter.

Wade and Sweeny had built an ice house, and they learned how to cut ice in the winter and put it in the ice house to keep food during the hot summer months. They were learning from the time they got up in the morning until they said their prayers at night.

Because the kids were with Miss Parker at school. This allowed Penny and Judith time to do other things, to sew, to can, to garden. Being that Judith was getting heavy with child, it gave her time to rest and prepare for a new baby. Chet wanted a little brother, Sarah wanted a little sister. Judith just wanted it to be healthy.

When the time came, Jake rode Golden, his pony to fetch Judith's mother, who assisted by Penny delivered the baby. It was a little girl, they named her after Wade's mother, Martha. But it wasn't long and she was nicknamed, Squirt. The first time her uncle Kemp saw her, he said, "She sure is a little Squirt, isn't she?" The same evening when she was getting her diaper charged, Chet was standing over her watching the whole operation and she decided she needed to pee. Grandma Sarah, who was changing her said, "Watch out she doesn't squirt on you." From that day, she was "Squirt".

CHAPTER FOURTEEN

Tim and Tom had taken a bath the night before. This morning they put on clean clothes, saddled up and headed to Denver. They wanted to see Val and Megan, take them to dinner tonight and go to church with them Sunday morning. It had been almost a month since they had seen them. They loved Eagle Valley and the people but they hated that it was so far from Denver and the girls.

Denver seemed to be busier than ever. People hurrying to take care of their business. The boys were in a hurry too, in a hurry to see their girls. They had talked on the way, they would split up and go see the girls and meet for dinner at the Windsor Hotel on the corner of 18th and Larimer streets, one of Denver's finest.

In 1863 fire had destroyed much of downtown Denver, the old wooden frame buildings were burned down. As a result of this, the new buildings were built of brick and were much larger, nicer. The boys had no interest in the cribs on Market Street or the bars and gambling joints. They worked too hard for their money to throw it away.

Tom found Val without any problem and she was excited to go to dinner. She had to first check with her parents, so Tom waited nervously while she did that. Her father was an undertaker and the funeral parlor was attached to their home. They agreed if they had an early dinner and she was home before dark. She told Tom the good news and hurried to get ready.

Tim found Megan helping her father in the store, and he too got good news, she could join them for dinner, but with one difference. Megan's folks would also have dinner at the Windsor Hotel.

The dining room at the Windsor was a little plusher than Tom and Tim were accustomed to, and each meal was a dollar but they felt it was worth it. Rooms at the Windsor were two dollars a night, they were staying at the Frontier, which was just a dollar a night. So their night out would cost them each three dollars plus the tip for the waitress.

It was difficult at times keeping the conversation going, but Val managed to keep them all relaxed while they ate dinner. She was more interested in what was going on at the table than of her own thoughts and feelings. This helped Megan as she was still struggling to get comfortable being in Tim's company.

After dinner, as they were walking off the porch of the hotel, they heard three gun shots coming from Market Street. The first and third sounded the same, the middle shot sounded as if it had come from a smaller caliber pistol.

"Ah, business for my daddy, maybe I can talk him into buying me the dress you got in your store window, Megan." They all laughed, but they all knew that it could be serious, gun shots on Market Street were all too common.

The boys walked the girls home and got instructions on when to be at the church in the morning. They had a Sunday school class before the service that the girls wanted them to attend.

On their way back to the hotel, they talked of going for a beer and then decided to call it a night. It had been a long day and they had already spent enough money for one day. Neither of them liked to drink that much and they didn't need to walk into any trouble.

They were up early and had breakfast in the hotel dining room, it wasn't as nice as the Windsor but it would do. They both had biscuits and gravy with bacon and coffee. It cost them twenty-five cents each and they both gave the waitress a nickel tip.

They were at the church early but the wait went fast as they watched some young boys play ball. They had a cloth ball and an axe handle to hit it with. They played what they called, work up. Whenever a batter made an out, he would go to the outfield and everyone would move up one position. The second baseman would go to first, the first baseman to pitcher, and the pitcher to batter. They had three bases and what they called home plate where the batter stood.

Tom and Tim had never seen the game before but it looked like fun. One of the boys, bigger than the others could really hit the ball far. He never seemed to make an out and was still one of the batters when the girls came to get them for Sunday school.

After Sunday school and the church service, they had a pot luck dinner. When it was time for them to leave, the girls wanted to ride a ways with them, but their parents said, "No". So they said good bye and the boys headed back to Eagle Valley.

Tim had picked up an old newspaper in the hotel lobby that somebody has discarded. He didn't read the best, but he did make out the reward poster in it for Jesse and Frank James. Two thousand dollars, dead or alive. There was also a story about some woman, Susan B. Anthony, being fined a hundred dollars for voting for president. The cartoon was of President Grant pursing the Kl Klux Klan in South Carolina. On one of the inside pages was: Wanted. A good firm woman to cook and help build a cabin. She should be able to skin a deer and tan the hide. Needs to own a gun. Send tintype of gun.

CHAPTER FIFTEEN

"Sweeny, I'm going to take Tom and Tim and push the cattle up toward our buildings, so it will be easier to feed them hay. Looks like we could be getting some winter one of these days."

"Okay, Wade. I will have Jake help me set up the feeders and think I will go ahead and put the wood burner in the tank. Last year I waited until it was cold and ice covered."

The fall weather was turning colder, the aspen had sled most of their leaves, all the animals had begun to prepare for winter, it had been days since they had seen a bear. The Sandhill Cranes had long flown south, the Eagles tend to wait a little longer before they migrate. The Eagles are daytime fliers, they typically mate for life and return each spring to often use the same nest as the year before.

Judith had packed a lunch for Wade and the boys. They would ride down the north side of the valley and push the cattle away from the tree line out into the open and then ride back along the south tree line pushing the cattle ahead of them. It would be slow work and could take most of the day. The cattle could sense a change of the weather and were restless.

It was chilly with the north wind blowing but still nice in the sun out of the wind. It had been near freezing early this morning when they saddled up, so they were dressed warm and all were wearing heavy leather chaps to protect their legs from the brush. After lunch Wade noticed the sky to the north was beginning to cloud up, getting darker. He felt they had most of the cattle from the north bank, and they could start back up the south bank pushing the cattle ahead of them. The cattle looked in good shape, they had good grazing and it did not appear that they lost too many to the bear and wolves. He had seen a couple signs of where a large animal had been killed and one was definitely that of a cow.

The wind had picked up and the temperature was dropping. They were still miles from home and the cattle sensing the change of weather didn't want to be out in the open. They wanted to turn their tails to the wind and drift toward the south tree line of the valley.

It came up over the ridge to the northwest all at once. One minute the sun was shining, the next they were in a near whiteout. It was a Northern blowing in, the temperature was dropping, wind whipped the snow, and they were caught in an early Colorado blizzard.

Wade knew it would get worse before it got better, that the wind-driven snow would become massive drifts. It was a cross wind so they could not continue, they had to find shelter. He saw up ahead a large blue spruce tree, it must be at least 75 feet tall. Next to it, he saw smaller Limber pine trees. This would have to be their home for the night.

He motioned for Tom and Tim to follow him. The wind was so strong and the snow blowing so hard that it was difficult to talk. He dismounted and tied his horse on the lee side of the tree, the boys did the same. Wade knew they had to work fast to build a shelter. It was getting colder all the time. They not only needed a shelter but so did the horses. Without the horses their chances of survival was not good. "You guys cut some of the branches off those Limber pines, bring them over here." All they had to work with were their knives, but they all carried Bowie knives, they would have to do.

Wade began to cut the lower branches of the big blue spruce, he wanted to get enough room to get the horses in under the tree. He piled them up on the north side, he wanted to make a wind break. The boys drug branches from the Limber pines and piled them up on top of those Wade had cut. The wind was so strong that it blew them around but soon they had them piled horse head high on the north and west side under the big spruce tree.

Wade had them bring the horses in and put them on the north and west. They turned their butts to the wind and their body heat helped greatly.

"Take off your chaps and lay them on the ground, and strip off your saddles and blankets and lay them on top of the chaps." Wade had his off and laid them flat on the ground under the big tree. There was a bed of old pine needles that would also help.

"Take your poncho off from behind your saddle and we will see if we can fashion us a tent." The wind had blown snow into the pile of branches they had piled up forming a wall of snow. The snow was an insulator, with the body heat of the horses it was bearable. Wade wanted to start a fire but this spruce tree and the Limber pine branches were so flammable that he didn't want to take a chance.

Visibility was only a few feet out in the open, Mother Nature had the upper hand and they would just have to wait it out. He knew that the fingers, toes, and ears would be the first to show any signs of frostbite, but he did not think they had to worry about that, as long as the horses remained calm and they stayed under the big tree. That was another reason he didn't want to chance even a small fire and spook the horses. If the horses were to get spooked, they would rip this apart. He knew wolves would not be on the prowl in this weather and the scent of the pine drowned out much of their scent.

They had some of their noon lunch, so Wade passed this out and they ate as the blizzard raged all around them. You can't control the weather nor can you predict it, but you can do some things to survive. The three of them snuggled together under the poncho, it was going to be a long night. They had a poor man's version of an igloo, it kept the wind off them, and they were dry. Between the body heat of their three horses and their own, they should make it through the night.

Wade's thoughts were of Judith and the children, they would be worried. He had heard stories of people being caught out in storms and their bodies found the next spring. He hoped that Judith didn't go to sleep with thoughts of this on her mind.

He was proud of Tom and Tim, he had not heard a negative word from either of them. They had not complained or whined about any of this. He had grown to really like them. It was funny how things worked out, it could have ended in a gun fight instead of friendship.

CHAPTER SIXTEEN

Judith saw the weather make a change, the temperature drop and the wind pick up. When the snow started she looked out and saw Sweeny and Jake putting things away and closing doors. She went to the porch and waved for Sweeny.

"Have you seen any sight of Wade and the boys?"

"No, we even rode out a ways and didn't see any sign of them."

"I am worried, looks like we are going to get hit with a Northern."

"Yes, there is nothing we can do Judith but say an extra prayer tonight before we go to sleep. Wade knows what to do and what not to do."

"I know, but that doesn't make it any easier. I have never been any good at waiting."

"Well, take care of the kids, stay inside and let us know if you need anything." He turned to leave. "If this one is like most of the early storms we get, it will blow all night and the wind will go down when the sun comes up."

Chet and Sarah had a million questions, about their father and the storm. Where was he? Was he out in the snow? Would he be home before they went to bed? Well, would he be here in the morning when they got up? Did he have any food? Did he have a blanket? Could they stay up until he got home? How long would this storm last?

"Chet, you hold Squirt and play with her while I get some supper started. Sarah, you can help me." It was easier and faster to do things without Sarah's help but Sarah loved to help and in this situation Judith thought it would be best to keep them both busy until it was time to go to bed.

After they finished eating and doing the dishes, she thought it would be a good time to say some nursery rhymes and sing some songs. Anything to keep them occupied until it was bed time. Because the storm had blocked out the sun, darkness came early. The prayers took a little extra time as they both had to remember to ask the Lord to take care of their daddy.

The bed seemed large tonight, Judith was tired but could not sleep. The wind howling and the sound of the snow on the roof was enough to keep her awake, even if Wade had been lying beside her. But with him gone, it was even worse.

She thought back to the first time she had seen him, it was in Missouri. They were joining up with Wade, Penny, and Jake to travel west. She was still wearing all black, dressed like all the Amish girls she had known back in Pennsylvania. She thought he was Penny's husband. He was long-geared, raw-boned, his arms were heavy with muscle, his shoulders broad. When she found out they were not married, she still felt he liked Penny and that he thought of her as just a little girl.

She remembered at Fort Logan when Wade had been cleared of all the charges. She was riding Kemp's horse and she rode up beside Wade, leaned over and kissed him.

He had this bewildered look on his face. "Why did you do that?"

"Because you didn't." That was so unlike an Amish girl, they tended to shun individualism, embrace composure.

She thought it was at that moment that she made up her mind to make him her husband. That seemed so long ago. Three children ago. She thought she was going to lose him when he got shot by Johnson in Denver.

"He took a good hit. I'm going to have to get that slug out of him." The doctor worked with a probe, a slender surgical instrument, as he searched for the bullet. Wade lost all sense of time and space. He passed out cold, his face and forehead covered with beads of sweat.

She remembered being at his bed side for two days and nights, hoping and praying that he would wake up. It was during that time that Sweeny got up the nerve to tell Penny how he felt about her and found out that she felt the same about him. With Penny out of the picture she knew Wade would be hers.

She remembered the Valentine he made for her. A folded sheet of paper with a heart on the outside and, "Are you free on Valentine's Day?" She opened it and inside it said, "If not I am willing to go to $2.95." She remembered hitting him and telling him that he wasn't going to get the gift she had planned. But she did keep the paper, and she did gave him his gift.

She dreamed, waking often to hear the wind and the snow. Each time saying a little prayer for the man she loved more than life itself.

CHAPTER SEVENTEEN

Wade woke up still huddled under the poncho with Tom and Tim. He couldn't hear the wind. He wiggled his toes, they were cold but they felt normal, the same with his fingers. In fact his body didn't feel too bad, he was not warm like he would be under the covers with Judith but he was not real uncomfortable either. His movement caused Tom and Tim to wake up. One of the horses stomped his hoof and it sounded like a gunshot right behind them under the big spruce tree.

Wade lifted the poncho up and off them, the sun was just coming up. The wind had died down and it was no longer snowing. They had to saddle up and see about the cattle. Wade, standing up bumped a branch above his head and snow rained down on them. They had to exit to the south as the wind had blown a big drift and sealed off everything to the north and west.

They got their chaps on and took the horses out one at a time. Tom held Wade's horse while he went back in and got his saddle and blanket. Once his horse was saddled, Wade held Tom's while he got his horse ready to travel. They had to ride south and swing around between the trees to find an opening back to the valley floor.

The sun was just coming up but it was still bright on the clean, fresh snow, and they would be riding east, so in a few hours it would almost blind them. The cattle had drifted into the trees to get protection from the wind and snow. Many were still standing under trees, tails to the north and heads down. They had to rope many and pull them out onto the valley floor where the snow was not very deep as the strong wind had blown it into the trees. They found one dead cow, she had failed to make it to the tree line and was caught in a drift, frozen. She would make a good meal for some wolf pack. Wade said a thank you prayer that they were not in that situation too.

It was slow work, but gradually the numbers grew and before long they had a small herd moving down the valley toward shelter and hay. They would pick up one or two along the way, one they heard bawling before they saw it under a pine tree. Tim had to dismount, wade the snow, crawl under the limbs of the tree, to put a loop around her neck so she could be pulled to freedom. Another few hours and she too would have been wolf feed.

The sun was well up in the sky now and they could see nothing looking straight into it. They had to turn their head to the north or south and use their hand to shade their eyes so that they could see. In a few hours it would be high enough not to bother them. They had to keep moving, their horses and the cattle needed a drink. They had their canteens but water was all they had. The thought of a good hot meal drove them to keep the cattle moving as fast as the snow would allow. "Hello!" They heard Sweeny before they saw him, he was coming, looking for them. The cattle seemed to move a little faster now, as they followed the path that Sweeny had made.

"You guys look better than I thought you might. Judith is worried sick, she wanted me to come find you last night." "We survived, and so far we have found only one dead cow."

"I got hay and water waiting for them, put the wood burner in the tank and fired it up last night."

Colorado was nice grazing during the late spring and summer but the winters could be very rough on cattle and wild life. This was just the first storm and it had caught them off guard. The women had stocked up on sugar and flour. They had fresh meat hanging in the ice house, a cow for fresh milk and some chickens for fresh eggs. Depending on the weather it could be months before they got to Denver or Fort Morgan.

Once the cattle and their horses were taken care of, they went to the cabin for some hot coffee and food. Judith and the kids were full of questions about how they had spent the night. Wade told them how they fashioned some shelter under the big tree between sips of coffee and bites of food. "Mother Nature caught me off guard, I should have been better prepared."

"We prayed for you and I asked for patience but that was about all we could do."

Sarah just wanted to sit on her daddy's lap, she didn't really understand all the talk about the tree, the ponchos, and the storm. Chet being older was full of questions. He knew it was serious because of his mother's worried look and her comments to Sweeny. But, his father was his hero and he knew in his heart that he would be okay. He wanted to grow up to be just like his dad.

CHAPTER EIGHTEEN

It was spring, nights were still rather cold but Mr. Sun warmed up the days and melted the snow cover. The cows had started to drop calves and the mares foals. It was a fun time to be in Eagle Valley and see all the new life. The Sandhill Cranes and the Eagles had returned to nest and raise new offspring.

Tom and Tim were itching to get to Denver to see Val and Megan. It had been a long winter, the first they had ever lived so far from a town. They loved the people here but they missed not only their girls but the hustle and bustle of the city.

Squirt and Luta were both walking, getting into everything and anything that they could reach. Sarah loved to play house with Squirt but was not real keen on sharing her favorite doll.

Chet and Dusty were begging Wade and Sweeny for their own pony. So they could ride with Jake. They both had grown up with horses, in the saddle before they could walk. Sweeny had his old gelding that he brought out from Missouri. He seemed to know when a child was in the saddle and how to react. But he was so tall that Dusty couldn't reach his head to bridle him or the saddle horn to mount. They wanted a small pony like Jake had. The problem was, that did not happen very often with wild horses and never with Blue Eagle's foals.

Wade and Sweeny had talked and had made a mental note to look for a couple of ponies their next trip to Denver. The boys were so competitive that it would not be possible to share one pony.

Judith's mother had come over to stay with the kids while they went to Denver. Kemp came with her, he had not been able to get over much during the winter months, but now that spring was coming he was here more often.

Judith and Penny would drive the buckboard. Wade, Sweeny and the boys would ride their horses. They needed supplies and the boys needed to see their girls. It had been a long winter.

The frost was going out of the ground and in places the wheels of the buckboard cut in deep. Once they got down near Bear Lake, the road was well traveled and packed hard. They saw others, some coming from Denver with a wagon load of supplies and others like themselves, going to Denver.

Denver seemed to change every time they came. People were coming from the east daily, by train, or by wagon train. Some were still coming in hopes of finding gold or silver, some were just passing through on their way to California. Some were waiting for the mountain passes to open so they could go further west.

"You ladies go shop, we will get a couple rooms at the Windsor, and put our things in it. We will meet you in the lobby about five, so we can go to our room and freshen up before dinner."

Wade and Sweeny took their horses and the buckboard to the hotel stable. The boys had already gone to look for Val and Megan.

"Any horse trader in town you would trust to buy a kids pony from?"

The hostler at the hotel stable looked like a picture in the dictionary for the word, grandfather. Everything about him seemed to smile. From the engraved lines around his eyes to the silver in his dark brown hair. He seemed to find pleasure in taking care of the hotel guest's horses.

"Well, there's a reason they call them horse traders, but I reckon Max Miller is about as honest as any." He liked it when guests asked for his opinion on something. "He's got a small stable down by the tracks, just east of the train water tower. Got a sign up, ya can't miss it."

Wade and Sweeny thanked him and went to get a room. They got two right next to each other on the second floor. They took their things to the rooms and then went to look for Max Miller.

On their way, they noticed several police officers, some walking, and one riding a horse. Dressed in blue with a shiny star on their chest. They were wearing blue caps with a black leather brim, and carrying a long stick. Their pistol was in a holster that had a leather flap like that of the U.S. Cavalry. They didn't seem to be going any place, just watching the people go about their business.

"Seems like the law is out in force."

"Yes, Denver has changed from a small town surrounded by rural farms to a booming downtown. With that comes crime. And these are the first police officers I have seen since St. Louis." Wade pointed to a small sign hanging over the door of a wood frame, false fronted building.

They knocked on the door and walked in. You could smell the leather and horse smell as soon as the door was opened. A large man, with bushy hair and beard, sit behind a scarred oak desk.

"What can I do for you gents today?"

"Looking for a couple ponies for our boys."

"Can't help ya with that. Had a Shackleford Pony, came from North Carolina, but sold him a couple weeks ago. The only thing I got are two small mares, belong to a couple of the Sisters at the Mission on Colfax and Logan Street. They rode them out from Kentucky, don't need them and want to sell the mares, their saddles and bridles. Asking fifty dollars each for them."

"Like to see them." Wade looked to Sweeny and got a shrug of his shoulders.

With great effort the man raised from his chair and turned to go out the back door. Wade and Sweeny followed him to several small corrals containing a variety of horses, mules, and donkeys. He stopped in front of two mares, one a silver dabble gray and the other a Chestnut. Neither could be over thirteen hands and eight hundred pounds.

Wade and Sweeny crawled through the pole fence, checked out the mares. Neither were great experts but by looking at their teeth they guessed them to be five, maybe six years old. The mares let them lift up their feet, without pulling away. They reached up and rubbed their ears without the mares throwing their heads.

"Don't know their breeding, would guess they could be descended from Spanish mustangs, and think they are both five going on six years old." He was leaning against the pole fence as if he needed the support to stand.

"We got a couple geldings, interested in taking them in trade?"

"Sure, where they at?"

"At the Windsor stable, we can go get them and be back shortly."

Max nodded his head in agreement and turned to go back to his office, leaving Wade and Sweeny to talk and look at the mares. They were a little larger than they had hoped to find but smaller and gentler than anything they had at the ranch.

"Think he will trade even up?"

"Most traders like to get a little beer money even if they like the trade better than what they have. If we had the time, I think we could sell ours for fifty-five or sixty and make money on the deal. But we can't take the time to wait around to do that." Wade noticed the same police officer on his horse going back the way he had come.

Max looked over the two geldings, checked their teeth and ran his hand down their backs. "I'll trade ya for the mares and saddles for five bucks each."

"Make it even up and you have a deal." Wade looked to Sweeny for some help.

"I can't do that, you are getting two nice gentle mares, the saddles and bridles, I should really have a ten spot extra to be honest." He rubbed his whiskers with the palm of his hand, as if it were a nervous habit.

"We could split the difference with you." Sweeny held up a five dollar gold piece.

"Okay, you guys drive a hard bargain, the only reason I'm doing it is that I feel I got a buyer for these big geldings." He reached out and took the coin from Sweeny. "Come inside and I will give you a bill of sale and have you sign one for the geldings." After the paper work was signed, they saddled up the mares and headed back to the Windsor stable.

"If it doesn't matter to you, I would like Dusty to have the Chestnut, she is marked about like mine."

"Sure, that's fine, I think Chet will like the dapple just fine."

They got the mares put up and went to the lobby to wait for Penny and Judith. Wade and Sweeny leaned back in the big leather chairs and closed their eyes to catch a nap. Two men who were dressed like salesman were talking a few chairs away.

"I think women are foolish to cause all this trouble. Why would they want to be equal to men? They have always been superior. They don't need to vote, they can just tell their man how to vote." They both laughed.

CHAPTER NINETEEN

Wade and Sweeny were driving the buckboard full of supplies. Penny and Judith were riding the two mares. They hadn't packed any riding clothes, so they were both wearing new outfits. Wade wondered if they had planned it that way. The supplies were cheaper than he thought they would be, coffee was just thirty-five cents a pound and sugar forty cents a pound. The new lasso he got Chet was only a dollar. Judith hadn't had a new outfit in almost a year so she more than deserved one.

The trains coming to Denver daily made things cheaper than coming by mule train. The competition of more than one general store also worked out in their favor. He was happy with the trip, the mares looked like they would be just the thing for Chet and Dusty. They had a nice dinner and night at the Windsor. He did worry a little about Tom and Tim. They hadn't been there this morning to ride back with them. But they could handle themselves, they would be okay.

It was a nice spring day, the sun was warm, and the wind was calm. He let his mind drift to the new calves and foals being dropped back in the valley. They had made a count and had lost only five of the cows and none of the bred mares. They would have to brand the calves and foals. Castrate the bull calves before they could let them scatter out in the valley. Depending on the number, they sell all the steers in the fall, keep the heifers to build up their herd.

The kids were all waiting for them when they pulled into the yard. Chet and Dusty could not wait for Penny and Judith to dismount, thinking the two new horses were for them. The ladies helped them to mount, the horses were still just a little too tall for them. They started to turn the mares away from the hitch rail.

"Whoa!" Wade grabbed the bridle of Chet's mare and Sweeny had hold of Dusty's. "Where, do you think you're going?"

"We…we was just going to go for a ride…." Chet got out very weakly.

"You don't know these horses and they don't know you. I don't want to see you doing anything but a walk until Sweeny or I tell you it is okay to trot. I don't want to see you jerking them around or holding too tight a rein. You see that Limber Pine, I don't want you going past it for now." Wade pointed at a small tree on the north side of the lane about a hundred yards away.

He could see the disappointment in the boy's faces, they had far bigger plans, but knew it was important for them to learn boundaries. He had watched the mares coming from town, they seemed to be just what he wanted. He watched as the two boys turned and headed down the lane. They had shortened the stirrups as much as possible but they were still too long. He would have to get the punch and put in a new hole.

He had tied the new lasso on Chet's saddle with the raw hide the saddle maker had put there for that purpose. "Now, I don't want you to even take this off, until I am there to show you what to do and what not to do, understand?"

"Yes, sir." He wished Tom and Tim were here. They also needed to build a spot for their tack. Low enough for them but high enough so that it was off the dirt floor. They would keep them in box stalls at first, the boys would have to carry water and feed to them. He would show them how to whistle when they gave them food and water so the mares would learn to know their whistle. He watched the boys riding side by side, they were growing but they still had a long ways to go before they outgrew the mares and the saddles. Looking past them to the east gate, he wondered where the boys were and what they were doing.

At supper, all Chet could talk about was his horse, he had named the mare, Silver. Standing on a stool he could reach high enough to brush her. Dusty was a little taller but he too needed a stool to reach his mares mane. Dusty named his mare Honey. Jake had said she was a real honey, and Dusty thought the sun rose and set in Jake.

"I worry about Tom and Tim. What do you reckon happened?" Judith was clearing the table, Wade was still sipping his coffee.

"I don't know, it's not like them not to come and let us know they would be late." So many things and circumstances had been floating through his mind, he hoped it was like his father had always said, "It will be not as bad as you thought it would be but worse than you hoped it would be."

"You and Sweeny plan to go look for them if they are not here by morning?" The boys had become part of the family, they were not just hired hands.

"We talked of it."

"Well, I think at least one of you should go and check on them. I know you got the cows and mares dropping but they can do that without your help."

Wade got up and started for the door. "Where ya going Pa?"

"Going to see a man about a horse,"* Wade smiled at Judith as he walked out.

"Mom, what's that mean when Pa says that?"

"It is his way of telling you he doesn't want to tell you where he is going or what he is going to do. In this case, he is going to the outhouse."

*An expression my father, E.R. Wilbur, often used. Thanks for being an awesome Dad.

CHAPTER TWENTY

The cell was about ten feet square, with one small barred window and a bed along one wall. The mattress was stained and had a strong smell of urine. The bars in the window and door were flat riveted steel.

At seven-thirty a jailer passed a zinc bowl of oatmeal made into porridge, with a spoon, under the door. Tom took one look at it and was not hungry. His head throbbed and his mouth was dry. He touched the lump on the back of his head from the night stick.

He thought of the night before, he said good-night to Val and then walked with Tim and Megan to her home. They said good night and it was on their way to the hotel that it happened.

"What you saddle tramps doing messing with nice girls?" They stepped out from between two buildings, four of them, blocking the boardwalk. The one talking held what looked to be a police night stick.

"You scum need us to teach you some manners?' He slapped the night stick into the palm of his hand.

Tom's hand dropped to his hip where his Colt should be. The girls did not like them wearing their guns, so they left them in the hotel room along with their Bowie knifes. It looked as if there was going to be a fight, he didn't see any way to avoid it. So, if that was the case, he thought it best to get in a real good first blow.

The guy with the club stepped forward to take a swing, he had the club in his right hand, his left arm hung down at this side. Tom saw the opportunity to strike first, he stepped in and swung a right cross that landed on his left cheek bone. His right arm came forward but Tom was inside, his bicep hit Tom on the side of his head, the club falling to the boardwalk.

The other three were on Tim, one got behind him and grabbed his arms, and the other two were using him as a punching bag. Tom spun around and picked up the club off the walk. He hit the nearest one to him and sent him flying. He swung again, hitting the one holding Tim in the back. The blow made him let go, and Tim swung with an elbow, catching him in the ribs. It was about over. Their liquid courage had worn off, when they lost the advantage. They also lost the will to fight.

Tom stepped forward with the raised club and they scrambled to get out of range. He was just about to relax when a blow from behind drooped him to his knees. He swung the club but had no power as he lost awareness of what was going on. Everything was spinning, he made an attempt to fight back but instead he fell to the boardwalk.

When he got his senses back, he was being drug into the jail cell, he heard what sounded like a man talking in a barrel.

"That will teach you to pick on some kids and to resist arrest."

He was dumped on the bunk and the steel door slammed shut. His head throbbed, his eyes didn't seem to focus, and he lost consciousness.

It must be the next morning, they just brought what appeared to be breakfast. He looked to the small window to get some idea the time of day but could see nothing but blue sky. Going to the steel door he could see nothing but the wall three feet away. He could hear someone walking toward him. He must be the jailer that passed out the oatmeal.

"When can I get out of here?"

The jailer stopped and looked at Tom through the bars, he was young, about Tom's age. He didn't wear the blue uniform of the police, he was dressed in blue canvas pants and a flannel shirt.

"Reckon they will take you before the Justice of Peace before too long. He doesn't have but a couple drunk and disorderly, and a disturbing the peace to hear."

A Justice of Peace was not required to have any formal legal education in order to qualify for the office. He had to be able to read and write and win the election for the office. Most of the towns paid their law officers salaries from the fines issued by the Justice of Peace.

"What am I charged with?" Tom was talking to an empty hall, he could hear the heels of the jailer fade away in the distance.

Dressed in a black frock coat, ruffled shirt and black string tie, the Justice of Peace sat behind a large oak desk. His bifocal glasses low on his nose, he looked over the top of them at Tom and Tim.

"What do we have here officer?"

"Came upon these two that one," he points at Tom, "Had a night stick and was beating some young men with it."

"Do these young men want to press charges?" "No sir, when I came on the scene, they took off running, never did find them." "I took the club from one of….." The Justice held up his hand as a signal for Tom to stop talking.

"You are charged with Disturbing the Peace, being this is your first offense the fine will be five dollars each or one week in jail."

Neither of the boys had five dollars. They had paid in advance for the hotel room, after going out to eat with the girls, they only had a couple bucks between them. "If you would let one of us go, we could get the money. We only have a couple dollars between us." Tom's head still ached and Tim looked to be in worse shape. He had some swelling in his face and didn't seem to be able to stand straight. Their hands were behind their backs in handcuffs.

"They can't pay the fine, take them back to their cells." With the wave of the back of his hand, he stood, indicating it was over.

CHAPTER TWENTY-ONE

It was a long ride back to the valley, no one had much to say and every step of his horse, Tom felt like a bass drum was pounding in his head. Tim too was feeling the pain of the ride. His ribs felt like he had been kicked by a mule. They were both thankful that Wade had come to get them out of jail. Good days tend to give happiness, bad days give experience, and this was an experience they did not want to repeat.

"I went to the funeral parlor and Val said she didn't know. That Tom had walked her home and said they were going to the hotel. I went to the Frontier, they had a room there but no one had seen them for a day or two. So, I went to the jail and found that they had a five dollar each fine for fighting and didn't have the money, so they were sitting it out. Lucky I had taken a ten dollar gold piece with me, so I paid and got them released. We went back to the hotel and they paid the extra day and got their things. It was a long ride home as they were both hurting."

Wade sipped his coffee. Sweeny and Penny had come over to find out what had happened.

"So, did you ever get the story from the boys as to what happened?"

"They said four guys jumped them on their way back to the hotel. They said they were going to teach them some manners. Something about Tom and Tim messing with nice girls. Tom said the one had the night stick and he took it away from him, that he hit a couple of them with it and had it raised when he was hit from behind. I am guessing the police office saw him do the hitting but didn't see the first part."

"Looks to me like the boys got a raw deal." Penny got up to get some more coffee, Judith was busy with Squirt.

"I wish I could have sent the record straight, but there was nothing I could do."

"Wade, you can't always control or fix everything. Sometimes you just have to let it be." Judith came and put a hand on his shoulder.

Chet and Dusty were busy planning what they would do tomorrow. Silver and Honey had never had so much love and attention. They would sleep out in the barn with them if they were allowed.

"Chet, did you water and feed the chickens, gather the eggs?"

"Yes, sir. We got seven eggs."

Wade looked at Sweeny and just smiled. "Any problems with the cows or the mares?"

"No, had three new calves this morning, two heifers and a bull. That roan mare looks like she will foal soon. There is only one mare that doesn't appear to be will foal."

"The boys get along okay on their mares?"

"Yes, I showed them how to use the side of a slope, a stump, or to just pull themselves up in the saddle. Both the mares are real good about standing for them and waiting until they are ready."

"I would like to get the mares so we could just turn them out, did the boys clean out their stall?"

"Yes, and they gave a whistle each time they would feed or water. I don't think it will be too long before the mares know their whistle even if it is a little weak at times." He made a sound of blowing air between his lips and laughed.

Dusty and Chet came up to the table. "Dad could we ride in the hidden valley tomorrow?" Dusty looked up at Sweeny with begging eyes?

"No, don't think you are ready for that just yet. Want to keep you where we can watch ya." It was not difficult to see the disappointment in their eyes and on their faces. This spoiled the plans they had been making. The camp site of Dull Knife and his band gave them all kinds of adventures to dream about.

The boys went back to making new plans and Sweeny and Wade talked of what they needed to get done tomorrow. There were always more things to do than time to do them.

"The boys were worried about the fine money, I told them we would just take it out of this month's pay. Can you think of anything extra they could do to earn the five dollars each?"

"I'm sure we can come up with something. I talked to Kemp and he wants to file on 160 acres alongside his father's. Think I'll have Jake file on 160 acres just across the creek. Wonder if the boys would like to file or do you think they will be going into Denver to find something? Neither of their girls seem like the ranch type, but you never know."

"I don't know. They were happy to leave Denver behind them today. It is so easy to get into trouble, as they found out. So many drifters coming through and the new police force. Denver is going to have growing pains but there will also be opportunities."

"It is nice to have them to help out but Jake is able to do more and more and it won't be long before Chet and Dusty will be helping too. I think they will be fine until the winter comes. When the Eagles start to migrate the boys too may get the itch."

CHAPTER TWENTY-TWO

"The Cherokee were pushed out of their ancestral lands in north Georgia because of the rapidly expanding white population. They were pushed into Indian Territory west of the great Mississippi River and north of Texas. A group of them followed the Arkansas River north and west to the base of the Rocky Mountains and then northward. This was to become known as the Cherokee trail."

Miss Parker was teaching a history lesson, something that was always of great interest to the boys.

"A Confederate force made up of white and Cherokee Indians was one of the last to surrender in the Civil War. They agreed to cease hostilities on the condition of being allowed to retain their arms for hunting. Chet I would not be surprised if your father didn't fight alongside some Cherokee soldiers during the war."

Miss Parker stooped to pick up Luta, who was about to get into some things. She put him on her lap and continued the lesson.

"Before the white man the Indians would make raids against other tribes. This would contribute to a village's wealth and it was a way to acquire horses. Raids were also an approved way to demonstrate leadership and to display bravery. To the Indian, the bison was the single most important resource. Fresh and dried bison meat was the main part of their diet. They lived in shelters made of bison hides which gave them the mobility to follow the herds. Bison robes were used as a floor cover for their teepees and during the winter heavy outer clothing was made from the hides."

Miss Parker laid Luta in his bed as he had fallen asleep in her arms as she talked.

"The problem of obtaining food for the laborers building the railroads was solved by buffalo hunters. They keep a supply of fresh buffalo meat to the workers. The most famous of these was William F. Cody who was known as Buffalo Bill. He is said to have killed more buffalo than any other man. Buffalo hides were also valuable in the east as they made them into belts to operate the large machines. So a great many were slain and skinned, leaving the carcass to rot in the sun. This sadden the Indian greatly as they were taught not to waste anything. They were also taught to respect the bison, as it was so important to their way of life."

Miss Parker, stood up and pointed toward the door. "Lunch time, see you after you eat." The boys all got up and raced to the door, Jake as always, was the first one there.

"Dad did you fight in the war with any Indians?"

"Why do you ask that Chet?"

"Well, Miss Parker said that some Cherokee Indians fought with the South during the Civil War."

"I never fought alongside any of them, but I did hear about some of the battles they were in."

"Were you learning about the Civil War today?" Judith reached over and brushed the hair out of his eyes.

"Mostly about the Indians and how important the buffalo was to them. What's the difference between a buffalo and a bison?"

"I think the early American settlers called the bison a buffalo because of the similar appearance. That's a good question for you to ask Miss Parker." Wade looked to Judith for some help and got a shrug of her shoulders.

"Okay, take out your slates and chalk." Miss Parker stood in front of them, holding her slate in front of her. The slate had two rows of little wooden balls on wires across the top. The balls, about the size of an acorn were alternately black and white, with ten balls in each row.

"Won't you tell us more about the Indians and the buffalo?"

"No, it is time for some arithmetic, get your slates and chalk."

"Chet and Dusty, count out loud as I slid the balls from one side to the other. Ready, Go!" Miss Parker would take a ball and slide it on the wire as they counted.

"Good, now Jake, you count by five's as I slide the balls." Chet and Dusty watched as Jake counted by fives."

"Now, Chet and Dusty. Look up here. I have three balls and I slide two more over by them, write the total on your slate." She walked forward to see what they had written. "Good, now Jake, you tell me how many I have counting by five's"

"Twenty-five?"

"Yes Jake, but your answer should not be in the form of a question. Say it like you are confident of your answer."

The arithmetic continued with Chet and Dusty writing their answers on their slates and Jake saying his out loud. When Chet and Dusty got to the level that Jake was at, they would pick it up faster, at least that was Miss Parker's plan.

"Okay, let sing the alphabet song." They all sang the song together.

"Good, now Chet, you say the first letter and when I nod my head, Dusty you say the second letter, Chet the third, and so on. Jake when they say the letter, I want you to give me the phonetic sound."

They went through the alphabet twice, Chet and Dusty didn't realize they were also learning the phonetic sounds the letters make.

"Okay, now I will say the alphabet and in turn I want you to give me the name of a bird or animal that starts with the letter. Jake you will start, than Chet and then Dusty." This was a fun game they liked to play. By changing their order they got to think of names for different letters.

"A – armadillo, B- bobcat, C – cat, D – dog, E – eagle, F – fox, G – grasshopper, H – horse, I – Iguana, J – Jackrabbit" They were going very well until they got to the letter – U it was Chet turn. "Can anyone help Chet out with a bird or animal that starts with the letter U?"

"Uncle?" Jake said with a smile.

"Yes, uncle works, an uncle is a man and man is an animal."

They did fine with vulture and whale but the letter X stumped them.

"xeruo- is a small ground squirrel found in Africa", Miss Parker hoped the next time they played the game, one of them would remember the xeruo.

CHAPTER TWENTY-THREE

Chet and Dusty had been riding further and further from the buildings. Wade and Sweeny had checked them out and gave them permission to trot and lope the mares. This allowed them to cover a greater distance in less time. They had their chores and their school work, but once these were done, they could play. Their imaginations let them be anything from pony express riders to buffalo hunters. The delight in a ride in the valley was not only in the beauty but in anticipation. Around each bend, behind each rock may be a discovery, an adventure.

Today they were Texas Rangers on the trail of some bad outlaws. They rode with their eyes to the ground as if they were tracking some real bad men. They crossed the creek south of the buildings and were a couple miles away before they realized it. With their eyes to the ground, they didn't see what was ahead of them. When they looked up they were within twenty feet of a little black bear cub.

They were both smart enough to know that where there was a baby, there was also a mommy. A mommy that had just came out of hibernation and was hungry. They were trying to remember what their father's had told them to do when face to face with a bear. They both pulled up their mare and looked at each other.

"Running away is a bad plan, some bears can run faster than some horses. Back away slowly making yourself look as big as possible. Bears tend to be intimated by loud noises and dangerous looking objects. The good news is, they usually just want to be left alone." The words their fathers were racing through their minds. Both boys stood up in the stirrups as the mommy bear came into sight, they pulled back on the reins and told

Silver and Honey to back. The horses smelled the bear and didn't want anything to do with her. The big bear was still twenty or thirty feet on the other side of the cub. She was coming on a run, but once she got between them and her cub she stopped and stood up on her hide legs.

"Back! Back!" they screamed as loud as they could. The two mares were more than willing to back up and put some distance between them and the bear. Once they got to the point they felt it was safe to turn and run, they spun their horses and kicked them into a gallop. The ground was uneven, and this was the first time they had rode this fast. They grabbed hold of the saddle horn and held on for dear life.

It wasn't until they had put a thousand yards between them and the bear that they got control of the mares and slowed down to a lope. Their hearts were racing, pounding and thumping in their chests. It had been an automatic response to the sight of the bear. Their breathing and heart rate returned to normal, and the mares also seemed to relax.

"We have to tell that we saw the bear, she is too near the calves." Chet looked to Dusty for agreement.

"Okay, but we don't have to tell them we were so near and scared to death, do we?"

Chet laughed, it was easy to do that now but just minutes before it was no laughing matter. They put the mares in an easy lope and headed for home.

"Pa, we saw a big bear with a cub down by the calves." Chet was waving his hand to get Wade's attention as they splashed through the creek. Wade couldn't hear what he was yelling but could see that Chet thought it was important.

He stopped what he was doing and turned to walk to meet the boys. They slide the mares to a stop and jumped to the ground.

"We saw a big bear with a cub just a ways from the cows and calves." He was pointing toward the south where the cows and calves were grazing.

"Let me saddle up, you guys go get Sweeny and the boys, they are in Sweeny's barn fixing some tack." He turned and the boys looped the reins of their horses over the hitch rail and ran to find Sweeny.

"When we spot the sow we want to go slow and make all the noise we can make. We don't want to shoot her or the cub but we want to drive them out of the valley and down toward the pond where she can fish and find game." Wade and Sweeny were riding in front, watching the ground for sign and looking ahead to spot the sow and her cub. They could see the fresh tracks of Chet and Dusty. Getting nearer the rocks they saw the tracks change, and Wade glanced at Sweeny and smiled. They could tell that the horses were running hard here over the rough ground, and they could just see the two boys bouncing in the saddles.

It wasn't long before they spotted the tracks of the bears. The wind was in their faces so they knew the old sow had not caught scent of the cows and calves. They climbed a little higher and up ahead saw the bears.

"Make as much noise as you can, slap your leg, sing or whistle." The old sow turned to look and then hurried away, her cub struggling to keep up.

"Tom, you and Tim swing around to the right, we want to drive them up that ravine and out of the valley." A long, deep, narrow gorge worn by running water off the plateau gave them a chute to drive her out of the valley. Once up on top she would be able to see the slope to the south and the pond where she could find food.

It was steeper here and difficult for the horses. Wade held up his hand as a signal to stop. The bear could go where the horses couldn't but she too has having a difficult climb.

"Let's keep making noise and watch her until she gets up on the plateau." They yelled and whistled, slapping their legs. Wade thought about firing his Colt but didn't know how the boy's horses would act, he didn't want to spook them here in the rocks. He made a mental note to introduce the mares to gun fire, just in case.

It was a tough climb for the little cub but once it got to the top, they both disappeared in the direction of the pond. It was slow turning around and going back down.

"Lean back, keep your feet forward, toes up in the stirrups. Let your horse drop her head so she can pick her path going down." Wade was pleased, it had been a good experience for the boys. They had saved a calf or two, got the sow and her cub to a good hunting ground and no one had got hurt.

CHAPTER TWENTY FOUR

Kemp and Miss Parker were waving good-bye to Luta who was staying with Judith while they went to Denver. It was the first time Miss Parker had been out of the valley since coming from Fort Morgan and it was the first time she and Luta would be apart. Deep down, she felt Luta would handle the situation far better than she would.

They would go to Denver for supplies, spend the night and come back tomorrow. It was a nice warm spring day the shadows of flying eagles sweep along the rocky canyon wall as they drove out of Eagle Valley to the hustle and bustle of Denver.

She had a list of things that she would like to get for school. Teachers were always spending their own money to buy things for their classrooms. The going rate for a female teacher was fifty dollars a year plus room and board. Male teachers were paid twenty dollars a year more. She had been receiving five dollars a month and this was her first opportunity to spend any of it.

Kemp had not been to Denver in over a year, so he too was excited to see how Denver had changed. He had been told of the new police force and of how it had grown. He drove with his Winchester laying on his lap, his thoughts on the lady beside him on the spring seat of the bouncing buckboard. He had been drawn to her from the first day he saw her in the commissary at Fort Morgan. He thought that she too was beginning to take a shine to him.

Neither had much to say as the miles rolled past, their load was light and the horses were trotting as if they were free, not hitched to the rig. From time to time, Kemp would pull them up to a walk. They were in no great hurry so he would let them walk for a half mile or so and then let them trot again.

The nearer they got to Denver the more people they saw. They saw several prospectors leading one or two pack horses, hoping to find gold or silver in the Rockies. They passed a wagon with two adults and three children loaded with chickens, ducks and a pig. They were glad to get past them to smell only the odor from their horses again.

Kemp drove straight to the Windsor, he wanted to get rooms and get their things in before they did any shopping. The man at the desk looked at him with a question on his face when Kemp asked for two rooms next to each other. He had not spoken to Miss Parker about their sleeping arrangements but his little inner voice told him it was the thing to do.

Once they had their things in the rooms and the horses and rig put up at the stable, they walked the boardwalk, looking at the store windows. Coming to what had been a vacant lot they saw a tent that a traveling drummer at set up to sell his wares.

He had books, pins, buttons, ironware, spices, thread, needles, lace, combs, oak leaf cigars, razors and razor strops, Connecticut clocks and tin ware. He was even selling Kickapoo Indian Sagwa that the sign said would cure everything from gout to snake bites.

"Can't hardly be without a bottle of that." She touched his elbow and pointed to the sign.

"I will take my chances, if I came home with a bottle of that, Pa would never let me hear the end of it."

He did pick up a cigar to take to his father. Miss Parker was looking through the books. She found, "The Jumping Frog of Calaveras County, by Mark Twain. It was a collection of 27 stories written in 1867 that had been published in newspapers and magazines. It was used, but none of the pages were missing and for a nickel she couldn't pass it up.

Kemp picked up some lace and thread for his mother and a used belt and buckle for his brother James. He wanted to get something for Luta too but he didn't know if he should.

"Look at this, for just ten cents." Miss Parker was holding up a book. Ray's Arithmetic, Ray's Practical Arithmetic by Joseph Ray a Cincinnati school teacher, published in 1834. It too was used but in good shape.

They took everything to the peddler who looked a little like one of the villains in the dime novels. His hair was slicked back with some kind of grease and he had a thin black mustache. He was wearing a white shirt with a vest and a black string tie. He counted out their purchases.

"Your total is a dollar and fifty cents." He put everything in a brown paper sack while he was waiting for Kemp to count out the money.

Back on the boardwalk they headed back toward the Windsor Hotel. They had not eaten since breakfast and the sun was starting to sink behind the Rocky Mountains. They would do their major shopping in the morning, so they could load the buckboard and get back to Eagle Valley before dark.

"Give me a minute to wash up, before dinner." She had her hand on the door knob to her room.

"Sure take all the time you need, I want to wash up too, some of that stuff in the tent could have been most any place. Just knock on my door when you are ready." Kemp waited for her to go into her room before he went to his.

After their dinner in the dining room they went to the porch to sit and watch the people. The Windsor was on the corner of 18th and Larimer streets, a busy intersection of the city.

"I am glad Sweeny wasn't eating with us tonight."

"Yes, he could have taken offense to those two men."

Two men at the next table were talking rather loud about the Irish immigrants they viewed as drunks, ruffians, and criminals. How back east the cities were being overrun with them. They were glad that Denver did not have a large number.

The big rocking chairs were comfortable, the night was calm, it was relaxing to sit and watch the people hurry past.

"Miss Parker would you like to live here in the city?"

"Please call me Patty, or Pat, not Miss Parker or Patsy. No, I am happy with my little school, I would not want to raise Luta here. How about you, would you like to live here?"

"Ah, okay, Pat. No, in the morning I want to go file on 160 acres back in the valley."

"You planning to build your own cabin?"

"Yes, James has helped me to start getting some log pole pine. I want to look for a two man saw and a new ax."

"Have you picked out a spot to build?"

"No, I was waiting to…." Just than a group of three couples came out of the hotel onto the porch. They were laughing and all talking at once about something that happened in the dining room. It was difficult to make much out of it, but they all seemed to think it was hilarious.

"Just waiting to do what?"

"I was, I was just waiting to file first."

The night started to chill and the wind came up a little so it became uncomfortable sitting on the porch. The sun had long sense set behind the Rockies.

"Should we go to our rooms?" Kemp stood up as he asked the question.

"Yes, I am ready to call it a night, it has been an enjoyable day."

When they got to her room, she turned and put her hand on Kemp's arm. "I would feel safer if you were in my room with me." She looked up into a pair of surprised eyes, he did not expect this, and it caught him unprepared.

"Are you sure?" He said in a nervous stammer.

"Yes, I am sure." She wanted to chuckle at the look on his face but knew that would be a cruel thing to do. She didn't want to make this any more difficult for him than it already was.

CHAPTER TWENTY-FIVE

They were up early and had their breakfast in the Windsor dining room. Pat was all a glow but Kemp had not slept well, he had a difficult time closing his eyes say nothing of falling off to sleep. His parents had told him for years that he would snore and at times talk in his sleep. He didn't want to do either of them lying next to Pat.

"Thank you father for this food, that it makes our world beautiful and fertile, makes us strong. Amen. I will go and give the store keeper the list of supplies we need, while you go to the Land Office."

"Okay. I don't know where the Land Office is, I will ask at the desk." He was still nervous, uneasy from lack of sleep and this new unexpected circumstance he found himself in. It is what he had dreamed of, but now that it was happening he felt overwhelmed.

The hot coffee and good food helped to take his mind off his problem. She was so pretty, and seemed so relaxed. He was a work in progress, it would take some time for him to loosen up and enjoy his new found love.

The Homestead Act of 1862 allowed settlers to file on 160 acres of land. They had to build on it and live on it for five years and then they got the title to it. It cost ten dollars filing fee and two dollars commission for the Land Agent.

"In five years you come in with two neighbors that will swear that you built on this land and have lived on it five years and you get a clean title to the land." The Land Agent was happy as this was the first two dollars he had taken in this week. He handed Kemp a sheet of paper with the date and the general location of the land.

They had all the supplies loaded and had started out of Denver when Pat saw a small boy selling puppies in a yard.

"Oh, can we stop and look, I would so like to get a puppy for Luta."

Kemp pulled the horses over to the side of the road and got out the ground tie. Pat was already out of the wagon and holding a little black and white puppy in her arms. He was mostly black with a white collar and white chest. He had a white strip down his face and two white front feet. He had long hair but was not shaggy. He had two little tan marks for eye brows.

"What breed are these?" She asked the boy.

"Pa said they were sheep dogs, from down south. Some men brought a flock of sheep to the cattle yards. She had her pups and they could not take them. Pa fetched them home and I have been bottle feeding them. They are about five weeks old and eating table scraps."

"How much are you asking for them?"

"Twenty-five cents."

"Oh Kemp, Luta will just love it."

"Are you sure you will share it will him?" He chuckled as he gave the boy a quarter. It was the first time he had relaxed all day.

The puppy was curled up on Pat's lap, the rocking of the buckboard had put it to sleep. It was a long ride to the valley, they may have to stop and let the little pup do his chores. They had been driving for a couple hours when Kemp noticed two riders coming toward them. They were still a mile away but that little voice inside him said to be careful. Up ahead a way was a big tree off to the side of the road, he could see where others had pulled over, to eat lunch or relieve themselves.

He didn't worry when they were facing him, but he didn't want to drive past them and show them his back and the wagon full of supplies. He had his Winchester on his lap and he levered a shell into the chamber. When he did this Pat looked at him wondering if he considered this to be a problem.

He turned the wagon off the road and stopped under the big tree. They were still a hundred yards away, but they looked rather sad, down on their luck. That could cause even good men to do things they would not normally do. There was no one around, they were miles from any law office.

"Just don't stare or look them in the eyes, we will let them pass while I can watch them, I didn't want to stay on the road and then have them behind us." He got out of the wagon with his rifle, he wanted them to see it in his hands. He went to the front of the wagon and adjusted the collar on one of the horses.

They were almost even with them when he looked up and nodded, he noticed that one of them had a Remington rolling block. It was a single shot, they were chambered for a .43 Spanish cartridge. It was a rifle that was accurate at great distance, used by many of the buffalo hunters. He had hoped that they only had hand guns, with this rifle they could shoot from a greater distance.

They rode slowly past and Kemp got back in the wagon, keeping an eye on them. He had handed Pat the reins when he got out, she reached to give them back to him.

"A couple of owls."

"Owls?"

"Yes the Cherokee call white men with hairy faces and big white eyes Owls."

"You drive for a while, that way I can keep an eye on the owls." He chuckled more to himself than out loud. "Being down and out causes men to do stupid things. I want to watch them, unless they turn and look they won't know I am watching."

Pat slapped the reins on the backs of the two horses and pulled back onto the road. Kemp was able to watch for over a half mile before they disappeared over the hill. He knew the next few minutes were important, Pat had the team at a trot and the distance between them was expanding fast. He watched for sun on a gun barrel, or anything that would indicate that they turned off the road over the hill and was going to attack. He saw nothing, and it was only a matter of minutes and they too had dropped over a hill.

"If you don't mind, I would like to keep an eye on our back trail. I think we are out of danger but I want to make sure."

"Sure, I don't mind driving, the team about drive themselves, I think they know they are headed for the barn."

Kemp watched and saw nothing, it was not long and they were at the gate to the valley. He got out and opened the gate and Pat drove the team through. After closing the gate he took the reins and drove on into the valley.

It had been a good trip, so much had happened. His life was changed, he wondered if it showed, he wondered if his sister would notice. She loved to tease and could be a little brat at times but he loved her almost as much as he loved Pat.

CHAPTER TWENTY-SIX

Wade was at the table, he had the tally books for the cattle and horses out. He wanted to figure out how many of each they had to sell to pay off the loan. He wanted to get it paid off, cut the amount of interest. He did not like owing anyone money.

"What ya doin Pa?"

"Just pickin and flickin."*

"Wade Lee Wilbur!" He looked up to see an angry wife holding the frying pan she had been washing over her head. "How many times do I have to tell you the boy...." She shook her head in disgust.

"I'm checking the ranch books Chet. Tomorrow you want to go for a ride with me and count the bull calves." Wade didn't want to look at Judith, he wanted to change the subject.

"Yeah, sure, can Dusty come too?"

"We will have to check with Sweeny and Penny but I think it will be okay."

Chet didn't have to be called to get up, he was dressed and ready as soon as his dad was.

They had breakfast to a barrage of questions. He wanted to know if they were going to take lunch with them, if they were going to hunt or fish, who was all going, could he run over and see if Dusty could go, would he need his lasso. "You just eat your breakfast or you won't be going anywhere with your dad. If I had a nickel for every time you two got on my nerves...."* She got up to get more coffee and Wade winked at Chet.

---

* One of the many expressions used by my good friend Al Sinek

They rode among the cows, counting the bull calves. They wanted to brand and castrate the bull calves as soon as possible, before fly season. The colts would have to wait until after the fly season and their "bad boys" dropped. They wanted to do it as soon as possible because the older the animal, the more stress, the risk of bleeding was greater as was the chance of infection.

"Once we get these foals branded, let's move them into the hidden valley, don't want them to over graze this." Sweeny nodded his head in agreement. Horses and sheep with front teeth in both the upper and lower jaws bite very close to the ground and then jerk their head back toward their front feet, this leaves almost nothing about ground. Cattle have no front teeth in their upper jaw, when grazing they swing their head up and forward breaking off the grass an inch or more about the ground, this is easier on the grass

"Let's ride over and see when Jokob can help us castrate the calves." He was very good with the knife, much better than either Sweeny or Wade.

They rode a mile or two and Wade stopped and turned his horse to look back.

"When you are out riding you want to stop every once in a while and look at your back trail. It looks much different going back than it does coming out. Look for land marks such as that big Spruce tree or that funny shaped rock so it will be easier to find your way home." Every time they went for a ride or did a job around the ranch it was a teaching moment. "I can be there in the morning, will get my things in order today." Jobok was glad to help out.

The morning was bright and sunny, they had talked over the jobs of everyone. Chet and Dusty would keep the cattle bunched near the branding site. Jake and Sweeny would rope the calves and drag them to Tom and Tim who would put them on their side and hogtie their feet with a piggin string. Jokob would do the castration and Wade would do the branding.

They had built a ring of rocks for the wood branding fire. They had to heat the iron in to an ash-color. It has to be hot enough to burn the hair and the outer layer of skin. It takes a steady hand working slowly and carefully. The brand should resemble saddle leather in color after it

---

* An expression my Mother, Hattie Wilbur Watson, often used. Thanks for being my Mother.

is applied. Wade used the eagle head branding iron that he had made in Missouri, years ago, it was a very good likeness of an eagle head.

Sweeny was very good at bending hot iron, and he had made several attempts to make another branding iron like the one they had without any success. The blacksmith in Missouri was a true artist.

After the calves were done and returned to their bawling mothers, they took a well-deserved break. They had branded ninety-five calves and castrated fifty-two bull calves. Steers were much easier to handle and the buyers preferred them.

"I will fix dinner Sunday, bring your appetite when you come to church, we will eat before I preach." Jokob had a pail full of Rocky Mountain Oysters, he had saved the one's he considered the best for cooking.

"We owe you Jokob, when you're ready to do yours let us know and we will be there to give you a hand."

CHAPTER TWENTY-SEVEN

Jokob was the chef for today. He cut the muscle off and removed the skin and placed the Mountain Oysters in a large bowl of salt water for an hour. After an hour he rinsed them and put them in milk for an hour. The next step was to rinse them again and put them in a big boiler over the fire to boil for at least ten minutes.

He drained them and put them in cold water to cool so that he could slice them. He cut them in about a third inch ovals, dusted them with pepper, rolled them in egg and flour and fried them until they were a golden brown.

His wife had baked fresh bread and made a large pan of baked beans. She soaked the dried beans all night, rinsed them and then let them simmer on top of the store for a couple hours. She drained them, and mixed a cup of molasses, a cup of maple syrup with salt and pepper and cut up pork belly. James had found some wild onions that she diced and added to the mixture. The beans would bake in the oven for a couple hours.

James had also found some wild watercress and dandelion greens, which Sarah washed and flavored with vinegar.

Jobok called them all to dinner. "Lord God, our heavenly Father, please bless these your gifts, which we receive from your bountiful goodness, we pray in your son Jesus name. Amen. The adults knew what the meat was but they had not told the children, they did not want to spoil their appetite. They looked like little golden coins, you would never guess what they were if you did not know. They were crispy and tender, with a real good beef taste.

"These are good, may I have a couple more." Dusty held his plate up and Penny gave him two more.

"Music is not going to be happy when he finds out he missed out on this meal." Sweeny pushed his chair back, "thank you chefs Jobok and Sarah, it was excellent".

After they were finished eating and the table was cleared, they joined together to sing and praise the Lord. Jobok was a good preacher, he liked to tell the parables of Jesus, and he liked to preach of the good works of his Lord. He did not dwell on the parts of the bible that could make you feel guilty. After hearing him preach and pray you felt good, you felt uplifted.

"When are we going to get my church and Miss Parker's school built?"

"We hope to have it done before the snow flies. We get the yearling colts branded and moved into the hidden valley and we will be able to go to work on it. The building won't take as long as building the pews and the pulpit. We can move the desks we have now until we can make some new better ones." Wade reached for his hat on the hook by the door.

"I don't need a pulpit to preach, but it would be a nice touch."

"It would be nice to have an organ or piano but they are so expensive." Sarah longed for the piano she could not bring with her. "With the train running and hauling fright they could get cheaper. I even heard tell that a company was going to make them in Denver the last time I was there." Kemp looked to Pat, "I'll go fetch the buckboard if you and Luta are ready to go."

"Yes, that will be fine. Thank you for an excellent dinner and a fine service."

"You are welcome my dear."

Mr. Sun was hiding behind some clouds that had rolled in and the wind on their backs coming off the Rockies had a bite to it. Pat was glad that she had thought to bring a blanket, but Luta didn't want to stay under the blanket, he wanted to drive the team.

"That was nice, I always enjoy our Sunday's with your family." She put her hand on Kemp's leg. That was a love, hate gesture. He loved to have her do it but he hated how easily she affected his emotions. She had complete control over him with just the touch of her hand.

"How is Luta and the little pup getting along?"

"Great, the pup follows him everywhere he goes, and has even started to try to herd him."

"What did you name him?"

"Well, that is difficult to say. Luta seems to change it from day to day. But it doesn't matter what he calls him, he comes bouncing to Luta just to the sound of his voice."

"Sounds like you made a great buy, a gift that will last for years."

"Yes, I think they will be best friends." "Now that Luta has started to talk, will you teach him any of the Cherokee language?"

"Not at first, but I do want him to feel good about who he is. I want him to feel fortunate to have both the Cherokee blood of his father and my white blood. I know he will act more white than Indian as he will be growing up with Dusty, Chet, and Squirt. He already tends to copy the boys mannerisms being around them so much at school."

"He will pick up things fast as he has some good teachers." Kemp pulled the team up to a walk, he wanted them to walk the last half mile to help them cool down.

"Would you like to come in and stay for a while?"

"Yes, I would like that." He had become very fond of her but often wondered if she felt the same or if he was just the only one around. Would she feel the same if she had more men to pick from?

CHAPTER TWENTY-EIGHT

The Kansas Pacific railroad that came to Denver had to be connected to the Union Pacific coming west from Omaha. This hundred mile line north to LaSalle, Wyoming followed the old Cherokee Trail. The Cherokee Trail from Oklahoma, across Kansas to Denver and north to just west of Cheyenne, Wyoming followed the Platte River.

The workers that built the track bed and laid the track were mostly emigrants from China. Despite their lack of experience with railroad work they handled most of the heavy manual labor. The use mule and horse carts to haul the railroad ties and rails.

They were paid thirty dollars a month plus food and lodging. They cooked their own food and many of them could save twenty dollars a month, which was a fortune by their standards.

In good terrain they could lay a mile of track a day. The problem of obtaining meat for the laborers was solved by buffalo hunters. Across Kansas they had a great supply of buffalo. That was not the case here in Colorado. They hunted deer, elk and bear which was more difficult and took greater skill. The Chinese's also liked fish with their rice, so they would use nets to seine the Platte River which followed their route north.

It was one of these hunting parties that thought a cow would be an easy target and a great change of pace for their menu. Wade was riding south of the buildings when the two rifle shots echoed down the canyon wall. He turned Eagle toward the east gate and gave him his head. His long strides did not take long for Wade to see a group of men just inside the boundary fence. They were standing over a cow and calf.

As he pulled Eagle to a stop twenty feet or so from the men, one of them swung his Sharps toward Wade. Now the other two followed suit, Wade was looking at the barrels of three buffalo guns. His hands went up to shoulder level as he studied the group of hunters.

"Howdy, you gents want to buy a cow and calf?" They all wore long coats, the front of their coats and pants were caked with dirt and blood from their past kills. It did not look like they had washed either all winter. The cow and calf were both laying on their left side, so Wade could not see the brands.

"Don't pay for an unbranded critter, this is open range."

"Guess you're right about that. You boys hunting for the railroad?"

"Yeah, you live around here?"

"Just down the valley, guess I'll be getting back to it." Without another word he turned Eagle and walked him back the way he had come. He had this funny feeling running up and down his back, most men would not shoot a man in the back for no reason. But that didn't make it any easier. He knew the blast of the slug would knock him out of the saddle before he heard the shot. He kept Eagle at a walk. He knew the men was more apt to take a shot if he was running than if he was walking. He needed to get over the rise that was just ahead of them before he could relax. His face was covered with sweat, he could feel it running down between his shoulder blades. Just a few more yards and he would drop out of sight. He was still in easy shooting range for any of the three. The shot did not come and Eagle dropped out of sight of the three poacher's. Wade took a deep breath and turned Eagle to the north.

He could follow this draw north keeping out of sight. He wanted to circle around and get in front of them if he could. He let Eagle have his head and the big horse covered the thousand yards to the north canyon wall, he turned him east staying in the tree line out of sight. Once to the line fence, he put his heel to Eagle and he jumped the two rail fence like it wasn't even there.

He rode several miles to the northeast, until he felt that he was ahead of the hunters. He found a good spot, put Eagle out of sight and waited. It wasn't long and he heard the sound of shod horses. He drew his Colt, wishing that he also had the big shotgun pistol with him. He didn't wear it around the ranch as it often got in his way.

When they were within twenty feet, he stepped out into the open. His Colt pointed at the middle man's chest.

"Now, real easy, you gents drop those buffalo guns." As he spoke he thumbed back the hammer on his Colt. This was a sound that all men recognized and understood.

Caught by surprise, the three men did as they were told and dropped their rifles to the ground.

"Now your pistols, do it with just two fingers, I'm a little nervous so don't make any false moves, or this Colt is going to spit fire." Again, they did as they were told and dropped their pistols to the ground.

"Good, now you boys ride into camp and one of you and only one come back with thirty dollars. When you do, your guns will be waiting for you. If you're not back here in fifteen minutes, I will take the best of the guns and be gone. I am sure I can get my thirty dollars out of it in Denver."

They didn't want to ride into camp, unarmed and ask the boss for thirty dollars. They would never hear the end of it, even the Chinese workers would learn of it and laugh behind their backs. They rode just out of sight and stopped to add up what they had between them.

"I got twelve dollars."

"I got ten."

"Here's, eight more, you take it to him and get our guns."

Wade had the guns all unloaded and in a pile beside the road when the hunter returned. It would take him a while to pick up all the guns and for them to reload. By that time, he and Eagle would be long gone.

He saw Sweeny and told him about the three hunters and what had taken place. "I will tell Chet, you tell Dusty not to ride in that direction until we say it is okay. Better let Tom, Tim and Jake know too." He put Eagle away and went to the cabin.

"Here's thirty dollars for your stash." He handed Judith the money.

"Where did you get this?"

"Sold a cow and calf to some railroad hunters." I will tell you all about it later when there are not so many little ears around.

"Chet, I saw a couple rattle snakes between here and the gate, it is warming up and they are out of their winter dens moving around. I don't want you boys to ride that way until Sweeny or I tell you it is okay."

"Okay, more fun to go the other direction anyway." He was busy playing with Sarah and Squirt.

CHAPTER TWENTY-NINE

Chet and Dusty were riding along the valley floor walled on both sides with sheer rock over a hundred feet high. It was broken so that a man might climb it, if he had to. The smell of the Ponderosa Pine and Spruce filled the spring air. Mr. Sun was doing his thing and they were very comfortable riding in just a flannel shirt.

A cow and her calf were drinking at the spring fed stream along the canyon wall. All at once the cow was slammed with a violent force into the water, which turned deep crimson. The calf turned and ran as the shot rang out from the high bluff to the north.

Chet and Dusty turned their horses and put their heels to the flanks of Silver and Honey. The horses jumped into a gallop, heading for the buildings, some Sandhill Cranes that had been feeding in the stream took flight in the opposite direction.

Wade and Sweeny working on the new church/school heard the shot and went to investigate. They saw both boys racing toward them, both were yelling something but they couldn't make out what it was. The horses slid to a stop and the men grabbed the bridles.

"Cow was shot!" "Somebody shot one of our cows!" The boys were pointing back up the valley.

Wade and Sweeny exchanged knowing glances. Tim and Tom who had been dragging Ponderosa pine logs to the building site, dropped their ropes and came to check out the gunshot.

"Boys, I want you to put your horses in the barn, rub them down and take care of them and then I want you to go tell your mom's what happened. Tim, you and Tom take a pack horse down, field dress that cow like you would a deer and bring her up to the ice house. Hang her up and bleed her out. Catch her calf and put it in the barn, the boys will have to bottle feed it. Sweeny and I are going to have a talk with some buffalo hunters."

They picked up the tracks of the horse just outside their east line fence and followed it to the northeast.

"I made a big mistake yesterday, I should have just let it be. What is one cow compared to our boys. I embarrassed them yesterday, made a contest out of it. We both know that he could have shot one of the boys just as easy as he did that cow. We have to end this thing."

"You did what you thought was the right thing to do, we can't turn our backs on every poacher that comes along."

They came to the railroad tracks and followed them to the north. It wasn't far and they saw three men with a net, seining the Platte River. Wade recognized them as the same three from yesterday.

The track they had been following led them to a horse tied to the tailgate of the mule cart. They had a couple five gallon piles of fish already in the cart along with another seine and some fishing equipment.

"Howdy." Wade called and they looked up from their work of pulling the net to shore with several fish in it. They had pistols on their hips but the only rifle they had was in a scabbard on the horse. Wade and Sweeny had stopped fifth feet or so from the men on the river bank.

"Want to say I got your message, loud and clear."

"Don't know what you're talking about." They had the net on the bank, they let it lay with several fish jumping in it and turned to face Wade and Sweeny.

"Our boys mean more to us than all the cows in Texas. We don't want to do anything to put them in harm's way."

"Like I said, I don't know what you're talking about." The one doing the talking was the one that came back with the money yesterday. He was older, had long black stringy hair to his shoulders. He had a mustache and full beard that all but hid his mouth.

These men were buffalo hunters, and now they hunted deer, bear, elk, and all from a distance, with none of them shooting back. A gun fight was too risky for them as it was for Wade and Sweeny. Out here, miles from a doctor, even a flesh wound could prove fatal. Say nothing of bullets flying from five guns.

Very often fights came from "liquid courage," the consumption of whiskey. None of these five had any of that in their blood today. Wade hoped that a "cool head" would take precedence. Even if he and Sweeny were able to defeat these three without getting shot, it was more than likely that the railroad would send someone to get revenge.

"I want to end this, right here, right now." He wished he had used a better choice of words, by the expression he saw on their faces he feared that one of them would go for his gun. If that were to happen, it would start a chain reaction that would not be good.

"I want to give you back the money I took from you yesterday. Call it even. End it for good." He reached in his shirt pocket and took out the thirty dollars they had given him.

"You won't get any trouble from us."

The relieved look he saw on their faces almost made him chuckle. He knew it was no laughing matter it could have ended very badly for both sides. He rode to the mule cart and placed the money in the back.

"Oh, that horse has a loose left front shoe, you may want to take a look at it."

Again he had to turn his back on them. Sweeny was watching for the moment but soon he too would have to turn and ride away.

It was one thing to kill a bison from several hundred yards away it took more courage to ride alongside it like an Indian and shoot it from close range. The same with a human. It was one thing to shoot them from long range it was something else to stand face to face with a very good chance that they would get a shot off at you.

"It cost a cow and a calf, plus a couple days of tracking but I will sleep better tonight."

"Yes, and I will feel better about letting the boys go for a ride, it would kill Dusty if he couldn't go riding with Chet."

"Just goes to show you how wrong you can be, I felt so good this time yesterday, with the thirty dollars in my pocket and not having to fire a shot."

"Well, for what it's worth, I think it will be a long time before they poach another cow."

"I will most likely will get some gruff from Judith too."

They were just riding into the yard, Tim and Tom came out of the barn to greet them. "Want us to put your horses away?"

"Yes, thanks." They swung down and handed the boys the reins. Wade was hungry and wanted to get inside but he wasn't feeling good about what he would hear from Judith. While he was eating he was telling Judith what took place. She had not said a word when he came in. She just motioned for him to sit and she gave him a plate of food and I hot cup of coffee. He explained what he had done and why.

She came around behind him, put her arms around him and laid her head on his shoulder. "I am so very proud of you." She kissed him on the neck, the cheek and then she bit his ear. It didn't draw blood but Wade felt like she had taken a hunk out of it. He reached up to make sure it was still all there. She never ceased to amaze him.

CHAPTER THIRTY

Wade was awaken by the sound of the rain on the roof, it was pounding down, like a cow on a flat rock. Both Cherry Creek and the Platte were formed on the high plateau on the east front range of the Rocky Mountains. With this heavy rain and melting snow there would be flooding. Where Cherry Creek and the Platte joined just west of downtown Denver would be flooded for sure.

He did not think they had any worries, both of their streams were spring fed and would not get the huge run off but they would get some and what was a gentle spring fed stream would turn into roaring water.

The wild animals would find high ground, only the nests of the Sandhill Cranes and quail would be affected. The eagle nests were safe and the parents would keep the eggs warm and dry.

The calves and foals were old enough and they would continue to get milk from their mothers, this could drain the cows and mares if it lasted for several days. They needed rain, they just didn't need it to pour down for several days. He could not go back to sleep, so many things raced through his mind. Whoever said that rain on the roof made for good sleeping had never seen the raging water that could come out of the Rockies and the damage that it could do to man and beast.

The rain did not let up, it was a torrent, a heavy downpour. He was glad that he had a poncho in the cabin. They would have to milk the cow and bottle the little calf. Give some hay and grain to the horses and cow that were in the barn. Feed the chickens and gather the eggs.

Work on the church/school would have to wait until the rain stopped and things dried up. A day or two of sunshine and it would to safe to ride a horse up the slopes to get logs.

Wade decided he would get up and fire up the stove to make coffee, with his mind racing there was no way that he could get back to sleep. He was happy to note that they did not have any leaks in the roof. The way the rain was pounding down, if there had been a weak spot, it would have shown up.

He lit the coal oil lamp and noticed that there was plenty of dry wood. He was glad that Chet had remembered to carry it in yesterday. It could very well have been Judith that reminded him, he was at the age where he needed a reminder from time to time.

The rain coming off the porch roof looked like a water fall, the yard like a large pond. He thought maybe it would be best if he just let Tom and Tim take care of things, they knew what to do and they were already out there.

The rain did not look like it would let up any time soon. He could hear the thunder and see the flash of the lightning coming from the Rockies. The sound of the thunder was two or three seconds after the flash of the lightning. He remembered his father saying that he could tell how far away the lightning was by the time between the two. That was how people knew that light traveled faster than sound. He would have to remember to tell Chet that when he got up.

"Coffee ready?" Judith even looked radiant right out of bed in the morning, he didn't know how she could do it.

"Just about, just have to let the grounds settle." He took the coffee pot off the stove and placed it on the edge to let it cool a little so the grounds would settle to the bottom.

They enjoyed a cup of coffee and quite conversation, it wouldn't be long and the kids would be up full or energy and questions. It wasn't often that they had the opportunity to be alone together.

Later, Wade was telling the children a Indian tale.

"An old Cherokee chief was telling his grandson about life. A fight is going on inside me, he told the boy. It is a terrible fight and it is between two wolves.

One wolf is evil, he is anger, envy, sorrow, regret, greed, arrogance, self-pity, guilt, resentment, lies, false pride, self-doubt and ego.

The other wolf is good, he is joy, peace, love, hope, kindness, generosity, truth, compassion and faith. This same fight is going inside you and inside every person. The grandson thought about it for a minute and then asked his grandfather. Which wolf with win? The old chief simply replied, the one you feed."*

*Author unknown, possibly a Cherokee parable

Chet and Sarah both looked at Wade with an expression of what does that mean on their faces.

"That means that if we every day feed the bad wolf that we will turn out to be evil. We will have anger, and all those bad things. But if we feed the good wolf, if we show love, tell the truth, and have faith, we will be good and the good wolf with win.

The rain lasted all day and all night, and well into the next day before the dark clouds that had been hanging over the Rockies moved on to the east. Wade had not been out of the cabin and he was beginning to get a bad case of cabin fever. He was not built for this and he was about all out of stories to tell the kids.

"I am going to go check on the stock, that little creek looks like the Mississippi River, want to see if I can spot any damage."

"Can I come too?"

"No Chet, I don't want you getting your boots all wet and muddy, that pair is all that fit you."

"Sure, leave me here alone, tell ya what, you stay and tell stories and I will go check things out." Judith had that look on her face that he had come to know so well. No matter what he said or did next, it would be wrong.

CHAPTER THIRTY-ONE

The rain had not done any great damage in the valley, they did not find any dead cows, calves, horses or foals. They had all made it to the high ground to wait out the storm.

This was not the case just west of the Denver downtown. People had built houses on what previously had been the site of seasonal encampments of the Cheyenne and Arapaho Indians. The key word being, seasonal. The Indians did not use these sites in the spring of the year as they lay between Cheery Creek and the Platte. Surrounded by steep bluffs to the foothills of the Rockies, once every few years they would be hit with raging water coming off the Rockies.

That is what happened this spring and it had done enormous damage to the buildings. A number of livestock were drowned and the water was badly contaminated. The cleanup of the flood was still going on as they made their way into Denver. A slight breeze from the west brought the strong smell of the stench to them as they rode into Denver.

"Let's take the buckboard and our horses to the Windsor and get our rooms." Penny was driving the team, Sweeny and Wade were mounted along with Tom and Tim. The kids had stayed at home with Judith's Mom, Mrs. Schroeder.

They were still checking in when Tom and Tim came in. The Frontier and all the cheaper hotels were full. The people from the flood had taken all the rooms. After their bad experience, the girl's parents had said they could stay with them but neither of the boys felt comfortable doing that.

The boys hurried to go see their gals and the others went shopping. Right now it was more looking than buying. They would buy all the needed supplies in the morning when they could load them right into the buckboard.

James and Jobok were also in town with them, they had come in to pick up the organ that was coming on the train. It was a surprise for Sarah. They ordered it by mail from a family friend in Ohio. They did not even know if they were in the correct station, there were four different stations. Very often passengers had to transfer between the different stations to continue their journey.

James was waiting for his father, sitting on a bench in the large waiting room of the Union Pacific Railroad. Large arched windows allowed the sun to warm and brighten the interior. There were a number of people either waiting for a train or a transfer to another station. There were two nuns on one bench with their traveling bags. Two men that appeared to be salesmen on another.

"The place is getting over run with them," one of the men was talking loud, slurring his words as if he had drank a little too much.

"Ya can't even swing a cat by its tail without hitting a church of some kind. Ya know why you never see just one nun alone?"

"No, why is that?"

"One nun watches the other nun so she don't get none." He laughed so loud at his own joke that he snorted like a pig.

"I'd like to go someplace where there weren't any…" He never got to finish.

James had got up to tell them this was not the place to be talking like that. One of the nuns beat him to the men. She put a Derringer .41 short caliber pistol to his ear and leaned over. She spoke softly, it was difficult for James to hear and he was just a few feet away.

"My little Mr. Remington can send you to Hell in just seconds, I understand there are no nuns down there." As she spoke she thumbed back the hammer, the sound of this in his ear made him freeze with shock and fear. She waited a few seconds for her words to sink in but to the man it seemed much longer.

She stepped back and almost bumped into James. She turned and their eyes met, he had a smile on his face. "I was going to intervene, but I see you handled the situation very well." He noticed how young she was, she couldn't be a day over eighteen.

They both returned to their seats and the two men embarrassed hurried to get away.

"Sister Denise our mission is to educate the poor children of the frontier not to put a gun to the head of a drunk." The other nun was much older, and not pleased with what she had witnessed.

"I am sorry Sister Mary but you did teach us to speak in the language of the person we were attempting to help if we possibly could."

This drew a look of scorn and disgust from Sister Mary. She had great concerns about just how well Sister Denise fit into the order of the Holy Trinity. They were on their way to a mission in Golden City from the convent in St. Louis. Golden City was the capital of the Colorado Territory, a growing city of just over two thousand people.

Sister Denise Ann Fisher had come to the German Catholic Convent in St. Louis as an orphan when she was fifteen. Sister Mary did not know the details but her father had been a federal agent and was killed in the line of duty. She had no family and had asked to join the order.

Just than a man came into the station and announced that those wishing to transfer to the Colorado Central Railroad to Golden City was to gather their things and come with him. The two nuns got to their feet, picked up their traveling bags and followed him out of the station.

Jokob returned with the news that he had found the dock where the organ was and that they could load it and be on their way home. When they walked out of the station to their buckboard the surrey with the two nuns was just pulling out. Again the eyes of James and the young nun met, he did not know why, but he waved. She smiled and nodded her head.

The next morning, Wade and Sweeny were loading supplies into the buckboard.

"You gents own those two horses with that Eagle brand?"

"Yes, we do."

"I got a gelding from a horse trader with that brand. Real nice horse was wondering if you had any studs for sale?"

"We do have a couple of young studs used them on a couple mares for the first time last spring. They sired some real nice foals."

"Where is your place?"

"North of here about a half days ride. You interested in one of the young studs?"

"Yes, if the price is right and his foals look anything like my gelding."

"His foals look good and the price would be seventy-five dollars." They had talked about getting rid of one of them as it was difficult keeping the stallions apart and they didn't want them to fight.

Wade and Sweeny gave him directions and he made plans to be at Eagle Valley in a couple days. He had a ranch just north of Golden City in the foothills of the Rocky Mountains.

CHAPTER THIRTY-TWO

With the organ, James and Jokob had also brought glass for the windows. Most of the windows were fixed and did not open, but one on each side was a sash window, where the bottom half could be raised to allow ventilation.

The window in the end of the building, which would be behind the pulpit. Pat had made to look like a stained window. She took paper and made a cross. Using the red color made from the sand stone, she dyed the paper a deep red. She laid the paper on the pane of glass and took another pane of glass and put it over it. Kemp using wood made a frame to hold the two panes of glass together. This window was up high on the west wall of the church/school. In the morning the cross appeared to be a deep red, almost black in color, but when the afternoon sun hit the window it was a bright crimson.

The organ was in the southwest corner and they had placed a window in the wall to allow light to shine in on the organ. The window glass had some distortions when looking out, they were more for light than for viewing.

Most churches had one side for the men and the other for the women and there was no mixed seating. In fact many had a different door for the women and men to go into the church. There was no soft glances nor tender hand clasps. Penny and Judith had talked about this and they wanted to start right out in family units. They didn't know if Jokob would object but Judith said she would handle him. She knew how much he liked a good smoke and that too was frowned on. The women did cover their heads when in church. It could be a cap, a veil, or an ornate bonnet but they did not enter church uncovered.

Judith's mother, Sarah did not know about the organ. She had not been in the church since Jobok and James had brought it and the glass from Denver. When she walked into the church, she was almost in tears. Jokob had not seen the cross in the window, so they were both pleased. He felt the cross gave it reverence, a sacred appearance.

She sat her basket of food down on the floor and went to the organ. The first thing she played was the doxology. Jesus loves me followed and then Holy Holy Holy. She had no music, she had to play from memory. They had no song books but they had been singing these so they all knew the words.

Wade, Judith, Chet, Sarah, and Squirt on one bench, Sweeny, Penny, Jake and Dusty on another. Kemp, Pat, Luta and James with Tom and Tim on the last. They would have to make more benches as Music and his family would be sure to join them soon.

Jokob was almost at a loss for words. He was choked with a strong feeling of joy and love as he asked them to bow their heads in prayer.

"Lord God, heavenly Father, bless this thy home that it may endure forever. We thank thee for your gifts, which we receive from your bountiful goodness through your son and our savior, Jesus Christ. Amen"

Jokob took a deep breath and closed his Bible. He paused to look out at his family and extended family. He turned to look at the cross in the window high above his head behind him. "Today I would like to give the scriptures a rest to just express how I feel about where we are and all that we have. When Kemp came to me in Missouri and told me that none of the wagon trains would take us because of our Amish faith. I never dreamed that we would have all this. I remember a few times coming across Kansas that I wanted to stop and Sarah would not hear of it. I remember how I questioned Wade's judgment. How we were saved by the Indians, and how another group of Indians protected our things here in the valley when we were away."

He paused to wipe something suggesting a tear from his eye.

"I hope that Sarah can remember how to play 'Sweet is the Vale' as it expresses how I feel about this valley. May we never take it for granted, that my grandchildren may raise their children here." He paused again, this time a little too long and Sarah began to play the song he requested.

The treble voices of Penny Judith and Pat, the tenor of Jake, Kemp and James overcame the fog-horn of Sweeny and Wade. Tom and Tim did not sing, but Jokob's loud baritone made up for them.

"There is not in the wide world a valley so sweet
As the vale in whose bosom the bright waters meet,
Oh! The last rays of feeling and life must deport,
Ere the bloom of the valley shall fade from my heart."*

- Written by Thomas Moore, 1808

After the service, when they were eating, Kemp told everyone the news that he and Pat were going to get married. Now that the church was built he could spend more time on the cabin he was building. He was building in right over a spring so they would have fresh water right inside the cabin. He got some iron pipe in Denver and he had fixed the spring so that it ran into a large oak bucket and out and underground to the outside. He hoped to get enough pipe to allow it to run downhill to his barn that he would build.

He had bonded with Luta, when he was around, Luta was always right next to him. He knew he would never be a father to Luta but he hoped to be a dad.

The other big news in the valley was that Val's father had offered to teach Tom the business. This was a big opportunity for Tom, one he could not pass up, so he would be leaving once the hay was cut and stacked. Tim did not know what he would do but Wade and Sweeny didn't think the boys would ever be very far apart.

Jake was getting bigger and stronger and could do more things and even Chet and Dusty were able to do their share. It was a mixed blessing, they would miss the boys but they would have another sixty dollars a month, plus the food the boys ate. That sixty a month added up to $720 a year and that would buy a whole bunch of things.

The two families could work together helping each other on the big things like the branding and taking steers and horses to market.

CHAPTER THIRTY-THREE

The eagle is the winged symbol of many people because it is seen as the strongest and bravest of all birds. The Indians wore the feathers of the eagle on their heads and on their horses. The eagle and its feathers were treated with great respect by both the Indian and the white man. Eagles are often considered to be a spiritual messenger between gods and Native Americans.

The Cherokee have an eagle dance and a wing bone whistle is used in the course of this dance. The Lakota give an eagle feather as a symbol of honor to someone who achieves a difficult task. The Cheyenne thought the eagle was believed to carry prayers to the Great Spirit.

On June 20, 1782 the bald eagle was made the emblem of the United States because of its long life, its great strength and its majestic looks. It was not until 1787 the American bald eagle was officially adopted as the emblem of the United States. The emblem is holding a bundle of arrows in one talon and an olive branch in the other. There were dissenters, namely Benjamin Franklin that wanted the turkey to be the national bird.

The eagle represents freedom, living as they do on lofty mountains, the eagle has unlimited freedom. Soaring on thermal currents it can spot game from great distances. Its main diet is fish, they will also eat ducks, rabbits, raccoons, beavers, prairie dogs, jack rabbits, sand hill cranes, blue heron, quail, even turtle and snakes. They have been known to kill and eat a great horned owl if it gets too near their nest.

Their nests are large, with a four foot or larger diameter, made of sticks or tree branches. They prefer the taller trees, the Spruce or Ponderosa pine. The nest is built in the top quarter of the tree next to the trunk where the limbs are strong enough to support the large nest and the weight of the birds.

James could see such a nest in a tall Spruce on the high south bluff as he came out the door of their cabin. Next to it was a dead Ponderosa pine that the birds liked to sit in. The sexes are identical in plumage but the female is about twenty-five percent larger than the male. They get their white head and tail at two or three years of age, and are sexually mature at four or five. It is thought that they mate for life.

James would often stand and watch the eagles. The eagle is sensitive to man and man's activity while nesting but at this distance they showed no sign of fear. Just over the bluff was a large pond or small lake where the birds could fish. They would also fish in the trout streams in the valley and once in a while they would fly to the Platte for a big carp or shad.

James had something else on his mind. The nun he saw at the train station. All sorts of questions raced through his mind about her. She did not act like any nun he had ever seen. She handled that little palm gun like she knew what she was doing. She seemed to be as comfortable with it as she was saying her evening prayer. How old was she he wondered. She was going to Golden City.

Golden City, that is near where the guy that came and bought the young stud had his ranch. He was there working on the church the day he came. He had heard them talking. Golden City couldn't be that far away. He had never been there but he had heard his father and others talk about it being the capital of the territory.

He was as old as Tom and Tim and they went to town by themselves, he guessed he too was old enough. He had to think of a reason to go. He couldn't tell them that he wanted to go see if he could find where that young nun was. His boots were getting a little tight and worn, maybe he could use that as an excuse. He could say he wanted to get a new pair of boots, and a new shirt for Kemp's wedding.

He had some money saved up, but what if his mom or dad wanted to go. He could just go and leave a note telling them where he had gone. Maybe he could tell them he was going over to Judith's and that he might stay the night. He was not good at this deceiving stuff. If they took one look at him they would know he was lying.

This was going to take some thinking. He looked up to see one of the eagles take off from the dead tree. The eagle got up and was soaring on the thermal currents, in just a few seconds it was just a speck in the sky. He wished he could do that, he could fly to Golden City and be back before they even knew he was gone.

"Mom, I am going to ride over and visit Judith. Will see if I can fix that shutter that rattles in the church."

"OK, say hello and give the kids hugs from me."

James liked to visit the Wilbur's. The kids were always so glad to see their uncle and Wade and Judith always made him feel so welcome. His sister could be a pest at times, she liked to tease her little brother.

"Okay James, what is it?" Wade had asked James to come help him in the barn.

"Huh, what do you mean?"

"You have been here an hour, and I know there is something on your mind that you are not saying. Didn't know if it was something you didn't want to say in front of the kids or maybe your sister."

"Yah, no. I just wanted to stop in and visit and maybe fix that shutter that rattles in the church."

"James?"

James looked at Wade. He didn't know if he should say anything, and if so how much. He knew that Wade and Judith shared everything, they had no secrets from each other.

"When I was waiting for dad in the train station, I saw this girl. She was waiting to transfer to go to Golden City."

"Did you get her name?"

"No." He paused and looked at his feet. "I think she….I think she will be at the school."

"And you would like to go check without anyone knowing?"

"Yes."

Wade gave the cow some hay and took a shovel to clean up behind her. He was trying to think of something to help James. James was shifting his weight from one foot to the other, wishing he hadn't said anything to anyone.

"I could go check on that stud we sold, see if he would be interested in any more stock. You could ride with me. Just to check out the country being that you have never been there."

"Would you do that?"

"Yeah, but I will have to tell Judith. But if I ask her not to say anything she won't. I am sure she will give you a knowing smile, but you will just have to take it and not say anything."

James looked at Wade, thinking about it. He didn't know why it was eating at him so, but he wanted to see her again. If not to talk to her just to know where she was and what she was doing. She was not like any girl or nun that he had ever seen. He couldn't get the thought of her out of his mind. In her black habit, all he had seen was this oval face, the laughing eyes that made everything inside him melt.

CHAPTER THIRTY-FOUR

"Sister Denise. Come in. Have a seat." Father Heilman laid the papers he had been working on to the side of his desk and smiled at Sister Denise.

"I talked with Sister Mary and she has some concerns, I have seen some of the reports of your activity. I felt it was necessary for us to have a talk before the bishop arrives in a few days." Father Heilman was not the picture you may have of a priest. He was tall, square shouldered, blond headed and spoke with a slight German accent.

"I heard about your encounter with the drunk man at the train station, and the man who was whipping his horse the other day when he brought supplies. You took his whip away from him. It is great that you can teach the boys to throw and hit a ball, and you seem to have a special talent to get them to do their best in their studies." He paused and looked to Sister Denise for some answers.

"My mother died when I was very young, my father who was a federal agent raised me. He taught me to ride and shoot. The Whiskey Ring case he was investigating in St. Louis for the Secretary of the Treasury was especially dangerous. He had given me instructions what to do if he were killed or for some reason did not return to our hotel room. I was to go to the convent, lie about my age. He told me what to say and what I was not to say. He made me promise to stay until I was twenty. At that time I could remain a nun or go back to public life."

The U.S. Secretary of the Treasury, Benjamin Bristow using secret agents from outside the Treasury dept. had sent John Fisher to St. Louis to investigate what he thought was the siphoning off of millions in federal liquor taxes. He thought it was a conspiracy among government agents, politicians, whiskey distilleries, and distributors but he needed proof before he could go to President Ulysses Grant.

It was a very difficult time following the Civil War. The industrial revolution was in full swing and children were the innocent victims. They were paid twenty-five cents a day, working twelve hours a day, seven days a week. Unorganized, abandoned by the government, deprived of any legal help, the children were power-less. Most of them come from the very poor or the orphanages of St. Louis.

John Fisher did not want his daughter to fall into this situation. So he taught and trained her what to do, should anything happen to him.

"What have you decided?"

"I am not yet twenty. I was not born with a silver spoon in my mouth like Sister Rachel.* I am not weak and unable to protect myself or to stand up for what is right. I very much enjoy the prayer time, the work with the children, and I promise to be on my best behavior when the bishop is here."

"You have explained a great deal, I now understand far better than I did before our talk." Again, he paused and began to shuffle papers on this desk. "Did you learn anything of what happened to your father?"

No details, there was a small write up in the St. Louis dispatch of an unidentified man that was killed in the street near one of the distilleries. I never learned more, I do not know if he was killed and if so where he is buried. I did what I promised him. I have thought and prayed about going back to St. Louis one day to find out the truth."

"Yes, I understand. Thank you, and may you hold unswervingly to the hope that you profess. Sister Denise, continue to do the Lord's work in your own unique way. I will assure Sister Mary that her concerns are unfounded. Please kept me informed if you make the decision to go back to public life, I would totally understand, as would our Lord."

Father Heilman stood up behind his desk as if it were a signal that their meeting was over and that she could return to her duties. Sister Denise, nodded her head and turned to leave his office.

---

* One of the many expressions used by my friend Al Sinek

With her hand on the door knob, she turned to face Father Heilman. "I will do my very best not to embarrass Sister Mary or you Father when the bishop is here. I truly do not mean any disrespect to the church with my actions." She took her vows of poverty, chastity and obedience seriously but she also had to be true to who and what she was. As she walked out into the court yard she looked up into the sky to see an eagle soaring in the thermal currents high overhead. She wondered what it would feel like to be so free, so powerful.

CHAPTER THIRTY-FIVE

Wade and James rode in silence, they had started out right after breakfast. He had told Judith the reason for their journey the night before and she promised not to say anything to anyone. But she also said that she would not lie to her parents. They both hoped this would not be necessary as they were not expected to visit. She would not see them until church on Sunday and by than this trip would be old news.

He was a nice day for their ride, warm but not uncomfortable for them or the horses. They were not on any time schedule so they let the horses determine the pace. They were riding to the southwest with the warm sun on their backs.

There were no fences, in fact the fence at the head of their valley was the only fence Wade had seen. All the ranches had fenced in areas around the building but on the open range no one had erected fences. They use brands to identify whose cattle and horses belong to whom.

The cattle brands were all registered. They are a unique marking that identifies the owner of the animal.

This practice did not originate in the U.S. the practice of branding was brought by the Spaniards. The vaqueros or Spanish cowboys played a huge part in the exploration and settlement of the American southwest. They saw bunches of cattle with different brands. A brand was read from left to right, top to bottom. Common brands, the spur, pitchfork, hat, rocking chair could be changed with symbols to make them personal. In the horizontal position it became "lazy", short curved strokes or wings added to the top made it "flying" and short bars on the bottom made it the "walking". Letters were often added with a number, such as the C3. A circle, slash, or bar could change it to make it different enough to register. Fights often started because someone would take a brand and with a running iron change it to their brand. The C3 could be changed to the Circle C3 by putting a circle around the C3 brand.

They began to see the Circle Cross brand of the man that purchased Eagle's son. They saw a group of mares with foals at their sides gazing beside a spring fed stream. They were all wearing the Circle Cross brand. Wade noticed that the mares were all heavy muscled, short but powerful looking. He now knew why the man wanted to cross them with the taller much larger black stallion.

They topped a small ridge and there was the ranch buildings they were looking for. They saw some activity in one of the corrals. The buildings were small but well kept.

"Howdy, step down. What brings you to the Circle Cross?"

"Just on our way to Golden City and wanted to stop in and see what you thought of the stallion."

"Boys like the way he rides, the ground he can cover in a walk. Anxious to put him with some mares."

They talked horses, the weather, and the market. The flood that had wiped out the west part of downtown Denver. James was uneasy he was eager to get going but he didn't know where. He had been thinking all morning about what he was going to say or do when they got to Golden City. At times he wished they had not come, at other times he couldn't get there fast enough.

"Well let me know if you want or need any more stock. I would just as soon sell to you as anyone." Wade swung up into the saddle.

"Okay, thanks for stopping in, Golden City is just down the road a couple miles." The man pointed to the south as he spoke. Wade turned and James followed him, still deep in thought.

Golden City was situated between Lookout Mountain and the two Table Mountains, in a sheltered valley fed by Clear Creek which flows from the west through town. They saw flour mills, and the only paper mill west of Missouri. The mill made paper from discarded rags and straw. In 1873 Adolph Coors opened a brewery in an old tannery building taking advantage of the mountain spring water of Clear Creek.

It was not large, and riding down Washington Ave. they were able to see most of the town. The sweet smell of hops was in the air. They saw the Colorado School of Mining off in the distance and the sweet smell of hops changed to the smell coming from the paper mill. They turned onto Mountain Road and James saw the Catholic school and church up ahead.

They rode up to the hitch rail. James had no idea what he would, should, or could do next. He dismounted and looped the reins over the rail. He turned to Wade, who was still mounted.

"I'll go get a sack of flour at the mill and see if I can get some paper for the school. You look around and I'll meet you back here." Without waiting for an answer, Wade wheeled his horse and rode away. James turned back toward the church and school. The church and school were built in a square, with a court yard on the inside. He could hear the noise of kids at play coming from an open field to the left of the square. It was blocked from his view by the corner of the building.

Leaving his horse he moved to a spot where he could see more of the play area. The boys were playing a game with a ball and a thick wood stick. One boy would toss the ball toward a boy holding the stick and he would swing it attempting to hit it. If he managed to hit it he would run to a spot on the field that looked like a folded sack. Than another boy would take the stick and try his luck at hitting the ball.

The girls were off to one side playing hop scotch, they had drawn lines on the ground and were taking turns jumping or hopping in the squares. He noticed the girls seemed to be watching the boys play their game more than they were watching the girl that was hopping.

There was a nun standing between the groups with her back to James. He could not tell if it was the young nun that he had seen in Denver. She appeared to be giving instructions to the boys. The boy with the stick, hit the ball and it bounced on the ground to a boy by one of the sacks. He picked it up and threw it to the boy standing by the first sack. The nun raised her arm with her thumb up in the air and the boy went out into the field and the one that was tossing the balls came up and took the stick.

James had never seen anything like it. The boy with the stick swung and missed the ball. The nun held up one finger and the boy tossed it toward the boy with the stick again. This time he hit it in the air but it didn't go very far and a boy caught it. The boys exchanged places and the game continued. This time the boy with the stick hit the ball high and far. He ran from one sack to the other and ended up back where he had hit the ball. Just than a bell rang and the nun clapped her hands. The kids all lined up, the boys in one line the girls in another. She clapped her hands again and the girls marched into the building and the boys followed. The nun followed the boys into the building. James almost got a look at the nun when she turned to follow the boys but her bonnet shielded his view of her face. He stood and watched until the door was closed.

Slowly he walked back to where his horse was in front of the church. He would have a wait, Wade would not be back for some time. He wanted to loosen the cinch on his saddle, let his horse relax. When he turned around, Sister Denise was standing in the door way, holding the door about half open.

"You're the boy that was at the train station."

"Yes." The word came out before he realized it was not a question.

"What do you want?" This question was very difficult for him to answer. He didn't know himself what he wanted.

"I just…I just wa….I just wanted to see if you were here."

"Yes. This is where I work and live. I am sorry, but I have to go." Before James could say anything the door closed.

James turned to see Wade sitting on his horse about twenty feet away. He went to his horse to tighten the cinch and mount.

"You didn't say that she was a nun."

Epilogue

The people living in Eagle Valley will continue to have stories to tell. Babies will be born, people will die. Some will leave the valley to make their mark in history. Others will join the valley family to make it even stronger.

Sister Denise will have a difficult decision to make on her twentieth birthday. Her decision will affect the lives of some of the occupants of Eagle Valley and make for exciting adventures.

The Wilbur's and the Schroeder's will continue to raise cattle and horses, to say nothing of strong young men and women. There will be new adventures and exciting experiences. Some dangerous ventures in a land still recovering from a Civil War, an industrial revolution and slavery.

Successive years of draughts and harsh winters will make life in Eagle Valley difficult. It will test the strength of the people and their faith in our Lord. The occupants of Eagle Valley will prove to be strong on both accounts.

Other works by Ken Wilbur

Blue Eagle:

A story of a young confederate soldier at the end of the Civil War and his black stallion. Their journey from Tennessee to the high plains of the Colorado Territory.

Eagle Brand:

Is the tale of three Colorado men who traveled to Texas and found more than they ever dreamed of.